EPIPHANY

Forgive me Lord, for I have sinned

Andre'a T. Robinson

This book is dedicated to my Mother Marilyn, Grandmother Estella, and the love of my life, my son Darrell.

"All that I am and strive to become; I owe it to them."

.

CONTENTS

ACKNOWLEDGMENTS

First and foremost, the strongest force in my life...My Lord and Savior Jesus Christ who I know is the gardener that planted this seed in my mind, and supplied me with the vision to write my first novel.

I would be remised not to pay homage to fellow author and developmental editor, Doris AC Johnson for humbly having faith in my ambition and talent as a *great* storyteller with respect to me being a first time author. She taught me and mentored me as we learned together and for that, I am grateful

Thank you to my Family and Friends for being a huge support system and embracing me at times of discouragement and self doubt throughout my life. I love my dear Sister, Tianna for always motivating me to complete this book. I can't thank my brothers, Robert and Ronald enough for being my rocks and holding me down.

Last and certainly not least...I have to send out a huge THANK YOU to my readers and supporters. Without you...there is no me.

~Andre'a

CHAPTER 1

... *IF IT ISN'T LOVE*

I despised the times when onlookers would suggest, "*...you should just leave.*" It was much easier said than done. There was many times I actually left, or threatened to leave, only to be drawn back by his deceptive charm.

In the beginning, it was heaven; gum drops and lollipops. I was blessed to have been in love with my best friend and then later, share in the joy of having a child. We were able to past down a third generational name to our son. He was named for *his* father who was named for *his* father. We were keeping the legacy alive. Family was important to us. That was my life. I met Carter at the YMCA when we were kids. I remember that day as if it was yesterday.

♥♥♥♥♥♥♥

May 17, 1996 was a hot and humid ass day. The temperature was one hundred and one degree's which was pretty common in Detroit. My friends and I didn't have many outdoor pools, except for at Rouge Park, and none of our parents would allow us to go anywhere near that place; the reason being that we were all only thirteen and fourteen years old. It wasn't that kids our age didn't hang out there; the bigger issue was that there were several different age groups of girls and guys and the guys were quite older than us.

We didn't have the appearance of typical thirteen and fourteen year old girls. We developed early and were fully equipped with wide hips, round asses, and big titties. Taking our "attractive beyond girlish looks" into consideration, Rouge Park was out of the question. Instead, we decided to go to the YMCA where there was only an indoor pool. I liked the Y (as we called it), because we would meet all kinds of people there and it was somewhat of a safe environment. I can't deny it; we had a few brawls up there with other girls from different neighborhoods and schools over the guys from their neighborhoods. It was a matter of territorial claim, but never anything major.

My friends and I were into older guys; but not too old. Personally, my limit was seventeen or eighteen… maybe nineteen years old, but that was pushing it.

I remember one afternoon in particular when we met a group of guys from Seven Mile. I don't know what it was about the Mile, but if you were from there, you were considered popular. The Y was on Seven Mile and Lasher so a lot of the neighborhood kids hung out there…especially the ones whose parents were concerned with their whereabouts and what they were doing. The Y was always supervised. However, every now and then, a few hoodlum kids would also come to the recreational center, but they usually caused trouble and got kicked out.

As we were all standing in line waiting for the next shift to open the only available swimming pool, approximately ten to fifteen guys approached us. Some of these guys were walking while others were riding bikes.

My best girlfriend Kristal knew the guys who were our age because they lived on the same street her Grandmother stayed. She talked, laughed and joked with them easily because they grew up together. In fact, their parents, as well as Kris's Granny, lived in the same house since before they were born.

I was quiet and had always been a bit shy when it came to boys. The guy who stood out introduced himself to me. His name was Carter Alden Jordan.

"Why are you so quiet?" he asked.

"Who me?" Bashfully, I continued, "I don't know, I guess because I don't know you."

He extended his hand and introduced himself, "Call me C.J."

I wasn't expecting him to be so polite simply because he was from Seven Mile. Being from that area wasn't necessarily a bad thing; it's just that we heard stories about the guys from that area. The stories were mainly about the older guys. C.J. was my age.

"Hey C.J., Sky," I rambled and then paused; "I'm Sky; nice to meet you."

After we shook hands, we realized that the line was moving, so we all returned to our places in line because that meant open swim had finally began and it was on a first come first serve basis. You absolutely had to be in line for entry. It was done that way because space was limited and only a certain amount of kids could be admitted. If you missed this shift, you would have to wait four hours for the next shift to begin.

I tried to hurry up and change into my swim suit when we were in the locker room so that I could make it to the pool before all the boys. Bear in mind that I was bashful. Although I received compliments on a daily basis from both men and women, I still lacked self-confidence.

I stood at 5ft 10in...weighing in at 155lbs. I was well portioned with thick legs, round hips, a plump ass, big breast, and a flat stomach. Older men told me all the time that I was built like a brick house... that I had an athletic build. I didn't play a lick of sports. I tried tennis but I had poor coordination. I attempted to run track but I wasn't fast enough. I was good at cheerleading but I felt I was too tall. I was more into English and writing...that's what I *knew* I was good at.

As I walked out to the pool, I was uncomfortable and afraid. I could hear everyone already in the pool so I tied my towel tighter around my waist. Although I was with my friends; Kristal, Tasha, Ericka and Toya, it seemed that all eyes were on me which caused me to feel even more self-conscious.

Immediately after arriving at the pool, I spotted C.J. We made eye contact. I believe he must have sensed how awkward and *out of place* I felt because he signaled for me to come over to the hot tub where he was while everyone else was in the pool. I walked up and removed my towel. C. J. looked very surprised. I feared that maybe he was disgusted at my appearance so I returned to being uncomfortable and put my arms around myself to cover up. I sat on the edge of the hot tub and put my feet in.

"What?" I asked. "Why are you looking at me like that?"

It took C.J. a minute to respond. He looked as if he was day dreaming and I slapped him out of his dream.

"Damn! I mean to say...WOW! You are so beautiful."

I was shocked by his reaction. I really didn't expect that to come out of his mouth...I didn't know how to respond.

"I don't know what to say."

"Well you could say *thank you*." he said, wearing that adorable smile.

"Oh my God, yes... thank you I'm sorry, I didn't mean to be so rude. I didn't expect you to say that."

"...so what did you think I was going to say?"

"I don't know, but not that." I smiled and put my head down.

I was sure that C.J. sensed my little touch of low self-esteem so he moved closer and sat next to me, and then he turned my face toward him with his hand.

"Sky, you are beautiful...never let anyone tell you otherwise."

I don't think I ever smiled so hard in my life.

After his innocent words of encouragement, C.J. gave me that *day dream* stare again. "WOW! Your smile, your teeth, and the way your eyes squint when you smile. It's so cute." he said just before he pushed me in the water and splashed it in my face. "...but don't let me give you the *big head*," he said.

I laughed and splashed the water back in his face. C.J. and I played in the water, talking for hours and getting to know one another. It felt like we were the only ones there... as if we had known each other forever and a day. I loved it because I enjoyed his company. I definitely hoped we would get closer.

On this afternoon, we talked about everything and I expressed things to him I hadn't told anyone...not even my mom. She and I were like two peas in a pod.

Before leaving the Y, we exchanged numbers and literally talked every day.

♥♥♥♥♥♥♥

C.J. was eventually kicked out of Henry Ford High

School during our sophomore year. He had no choice but to enroll in the school I attended which was Redford High School because it was the neighboring high school to Henry Ford High School.

For the most part, C.J. was a nice kid, but he was stubborn and hard headed which caused him to get into a lot of fights. He and I had that in common because I was explosive in the same way. In fact, that's part of the reason why we became best friends.

C.J. was somewhat of a *ladies man*. He used to talk to all my girl friends. Some of his flirtatious ways also attracted the attention of girls that went to our high school that I didn't particularly care too much for. I would get into arguments...often times fights, because they were jealous that we were so close. Everyone knew of our friendship but most people couldn't understand how we could be of the opposite sex and not be more than that...just friends.

I don't think we were attracted to each other at that time...at least I wasn't. Don't misunderstand me, C.J. was a handsome guy... and that smile, personality and aggressive behavior made him very attractive, but our friendship was important to both of us.

Our relationship was jeopardized at the end of our sophomore year when I started dating this popular guy. Troy was on our school football team. He and C.J. were from *hoods* that didn't get along too well; Brightmoor and Seven Mile were a bad mix of company. Aside from that, C.J. was originally from Henry Ford High School and our schools were popular for being rivalries. Needless to say; they hated each other. Troy couldn't understand how I had a male best friend...especially someone like C.J. who he was sure had tried to *get in my pants* before.

As for C.J., I didn't know if he hated Troy because of the *beef* they had being that they were from different hoods, or if he hated Troy because I was his girlfriend and loved him so much. According to my best friend, Troy was all I talked about. I admit that I sometimes dissed C.J. when Troy wanted to see me, but at the time, I didn't realize C.J. was just trying to protect my heart. I had no idea that I was an unsuspecting *fool* that did not know Troy was fucking seventy percent of the girls at our school (my friends included) throughout the four years that we were *together*. C.J. didn't want to tell me because he feared my response. He figured it could go either two ways; I leave that weak *ass nigga* or, I take it the wrong way and blame him. He didn't want to ruin our friendship so he chose to leave it alone. I'm sure he thought I would find out sooner or later...quite naturally, that is exactly what happened.

CHAPTER 2

BLUE SKY

After we graduated high school, Troy and I were together for about another year. He received a scholarship to play football at Michigan State University so he left to go to school early that fall. I went to a local community college because I wasn't too keen on moving away from my family. However, I would drive to Lansing (which was nearly three hours away) to go see him the times he did not come home during breaks.

I ended up getting pregnant between his trips to the city and those long drives to the University. I was excited about the news of the pregnancy and thought we were happy but little did I know someone close to me was also pregnant with Troy's baby. That *someone* was my best girlfriend since we were kids. Kristal was about six months and she had already shared the news of her pregnancy. I thought I knew who her baby's daddy was because she had been dating one guy *exclusively* for nearly two years (so I thought). We talked every day. In fact, nothing had changed with

our friendship since we were kids. When you saw me...
you saw Kristal. People often called us Laverne and
Shirley. We hung like wet clothes. I would often spend
nights at a time with her at her apartment...I was even
planning and paying for some of the things needed for
her Baby Shower. Helping her *special day* be a special
day was important to me.

When I found out I was pregnant, we agreed that we
would have our Baby Shower together. I found it odd
that she kept toying around with the plans. She
seemed uncertain of the theme, date, and location.I
soon learned why. The same man would have to be
present at the Baby Shower because we were going to
have the same damn baby's daddy and Troy would
have to show the world both of his two faces.

♥♥♥♥♥♥♥♥

I received a phone call from one of our longtime
childhood friends. Toya had gone into the military after
we graduated from high school.

"Hello," I answered when the phone rang.

"Hey girl...what you doing?"

"...nothing really. I'm sitting here looking at things for
the baby. What's new? What have you been up to?"

Toya got quiet for what seemed like a long one minute
and I was dying to know why. Maybe it was women's
intuition because I knew she wasn't about to give me
any good news. First of all, she was calling during the
week. The military boot camp program had strict rules
so she only got to call home on weekends unless it was

an emergency. I believe she thought she was justified in what she was about to reveal.

"Are you sitting down, Sky? There's something I need to tell you that you are probably not going to like."

Toya paused and sighed for a minute and began again, "Sky, Kristal is pregnant by Troy."

My chest felt like someone dropped a million and one bricks on it. I lost wind before I dropped the phone and started hyperventilating. I felt faint. As I stood up, my legs felt like noodles which caused me to drop to my knees. I had never had a heart attack before but I was sure that it probably felt like what I was going through at that time. There was a loud thump upon me landing on my knees.

I didn't know that my Mom, Step Dad, C.J., and my cousin were waiting outside of the door. Toya had alerted them all before she called me because she knew how I could get. I was explosive by nature but I knew how to react discreetly. This situation was different. Burning Kristal's apartment down wouldn't satisfy my appetite to make her pay. I was ready to dilate Kristal's cervix with the heel of my stiletto...wishing no harm to her baby.

Thankfully, Toya was wise enough to know that this wouldn't end well if I was left alone. Without a doubt, Kristal was sure to get that ass beat.

Toya warned my family so that they stayed near...it was for the best.

I was thinking that C. J. should have known me well

enough to cuff me to a chair for Kristal's safety. In the end, they didn't expect the reaction they got, but it was all I knew to give. The situation broke me down.

I cried for hours in my mom's and C.J.'s arms that night. My mom let C.J. spend the night to keep an eye on me and that is the night I started to have feelings for C.J. He felt the same way, and it was obvious in the way he held me as I cried.

C. J. intercepted the ringing telephone the entire night. He answered and hung up the phone for me every time Troy and Kristal called to try to explain themselves. C.J. didn't want anyone to bother me (especially not those two clowns) until I calmed down and got myself together. He sat me up in the bed and gave me a pep talk.

"Look Sky, I know you're hurting, but you are not going to let this sucka ass nigga throw you off your square. You're Sky! I know you love that lame. I can't do anything but respect that because you're my BF...my lil sis, but I'm not about to let you raise a child alone. Don't think that because you're pregnant, you have to take that sucka back!" Then he said what he always said to me since the first day I met him at the Y seven years earlier, except this time, we said it together (through my horse voice and tears), "Sky, you are beautiful and never let anyone tell you otherwise."

We busted out laughing.

"Thank you. You are the best, C.J."

"For what? Sky, you know I will always have your back."

♥♥♥♥♥♥♥♥

Ultimately, I decided to have an abortion. The decision was influenced by my Mom, Step Dad and Aunts. I really didn't want to do it but, I knew there was no way I could raise a child on my own at nineteen years old.

CHAPTER 3

ENOUGH IS NOT ENOUGH

The sound of Lil Carter knocking on our bedroom door snapped me out of my *day dream*.

"Mommy, are you ok?"

"I'm fine... Carter, go in your room and play your video game. Mommy will be out in a minute."

When I heard his door shut, I slid out of my room, across the hallway, and then into the bathroom. The living room was quiet so I figured C.J. had left. After I got in the bathroom, I became more afraid to look in the mirror than previous *encounters* because (by the way my face *felt*) I knew it didn't *look* good. When I got up the nerve to look, I didn't recognize the person looking back at me in the mirror.

My face was disfigured...covered in black and blue bruises. My eyes were almost completely swollen shut. His hand prints seemed masterfully embedded in my neck. I couldn't even cry because my face hurt so badly. It looked as if I was in a head on collision car wreck. I couldn't believe that I was standing there looking at myself when I probably should have I been in the hospital hooked to a machine and fighting for my life. I could have easily passed as someone who was in critical condition.

I was scared that my son was going to have to see me like this. I knew he would be horrified. I looked like a monster. Shit, I was afraid of myself!

I saw Lil Carter standing in the door way of the bathroom with the one eye I could somewhat see out of.

"Ma, what happened to you? Did dad do this?"

Sadly, even at his young age, our son was sure his dad was responsible for my condition because he heard me screaming and pleading for him to stop on more than one occasion. I hated having to explain these events to him because I didn't want him to hate his dad. Family was everything to me. Once upon a time, it meant something to C.J.

He cared less and less, and it was evident when the fights began to happen even when our son was home. C.J. simply didn't care anymore. Lil Carter would cry and beg for his dad to stop beating me up but he blocked it out and continued until his satisfaction. He would transform into being someone and something I wasn't familiar with...and someone and something I didn't want to know.

In his moments of darkness, C.J. would become as tall

as a shadow towering over me. The ice cold, black, demonic look in his eyes starred right through me. I found it easiest to fool myself into believing he was possessed when he beat on me because his mind would go somewhere on a trip and then he would realize what he had done and snap out of it. He would go from 1 to 10 and then after a while, return to being scary calm. I tried to find logic in his behavior so I use to assume that maybe he was schizophrenic. In my mind, he was anything but normal.

♥♥♥♥♥♥♥♥

Lil Carter began to cry because my face was starting to swell more.

"Mommy, I think we should go to the hospital."

I could see the fear in his little innocent eyes. He wanted to be brave but he said he was afraid, and hearing him say those words made it surreal. I was crushed as a mother to appear so helpless. I mustered up what breath I could to tell him that we would go to the hospital. Saying those few words hurt like hell. C.J. had squeezed my neck so hard while he was choking me that I could barely speak. Actually, saying that my throat was hurting was an understatement.

This particular incident was the result of C.J. cheating on me and the girl contacting me on Facebook. He would attack me for almost anything. Hell, the wind could be blowing too hard and it would somehow be my fault. Not only did he whoop my ass every chance he got; he couldn't be faithful if it was to save his own life.

Thinking about all this made me cry again. I couldn't believe that my life was heading in the direction it was going. I contemplated just ending it all so many times but I couldn't leave Lil Carter out in the world to live without me. I knew I would always protect and love him unconditionally the way no one else would.

With this in mind, I couldn't stomach going through with it. He was all I had after losing my mom to kidney disease two years earlier...and my dad was murdered in a high profile case almost twenty five years prior. Three months before this attack, I had lost the only grandmother I had due to pancreatic cancer.

The reason I considered her my *only* grandmother was because my dad's mom was never in the picture. I can remember going to her house as a kid with my dad and she wasn't exactly the nicest woman in the world. Usually when you meet a person, you respond, "It is nice meeting you." This was not the case with her. She was nothing like a grandmother is supposed to be. This woman had a hole where her heart should have been which made her heartless. Even as an adult looking back, I maintain that she was very mean and unpleasant. In fact, she used to act as if she didn't care for me *or* any of my brothers and sisters. She wouldn't talk to me... made no attempts to be loving and nurturing. I don't even remember her even once saying *Hi* to me. *What would it hurt to greet a harmless child?* Perhaps, I should have cared but surprisingly, it didn't affect me. Needless to say, she received insurance money from my dad's death and none of his children got any money or anything else from her for that matter.

♥♥♥♥♥♥♥♥

C.J. didn't come back home that night. Against my better judgment, I didn't go to the hospital. I could hardly see to drive and I didn't want to call anyone in my family because then it would be an even bigger issue. I knew Lil Carter feared what things might happen to me during the night so I let him sleep in the bed with me.

The next morning, I woke up to Lil Carter making noises in the living room. He was playing his play station. I continued to struggle to see out of my eyes however, I was able to get out the bed and make my way into the living room. It seemed the pain was even worse on this morning. I was stiff, light headed, and nauseous. And I *still* looked like the monster I saw in the mirror the night before.

When I reached the entrance to the living room, Lil Carter stopped playing his game and just stared at my face. He must have been looking at the same monster that I was seeing.

"Hey baby," I said trying not to cry. "Are you hungry?"

"Yes Mommy, but..." he paused because we heard the keys in the front doorknob, which could only have been C.J. coming home. Sure enough, in walks C.J. with breakfast and an armful of toys.

"Hey Daddy," Lil Carter said nervously.

"Hey son!"

C.J. couldn't even look at me and when he did, he

looked like a deer caught in the headlights. His facial expression was pathetic. It said to me...*what have I done?*

I turned to walk away and headed into the bathroom to get a good look at my face and when I got in the mirror I couldn't believe what I was seeing...not much had changed from the night before. I looked like Martin did on the episode when he got into the fight with Tommy Hearns...but a little worse. I was devastated. It still hurt to cry. I was crying so hard that I started wheezing because my throat hurt and my lips were so swollen I could hardly open them to allow air in and out. C.J. and Lil Carter must have heard me because Lil Carter came running up the hallway to the bathroom.

"Mommy, are you ok?"

"Yes Carter...Mommy is just in a little tiny bit of pain."

I didn't want to worry him. Where I came from, adults handled their own affairs and the children had no involvement.

When I looked up from hugging Lil Carter, C.J. was standing in the doorway.

"Go play your game Carter. Let me and your Mom talk."

Lil Carter looked at me with tears in his eyes and I reassured him that I would be fine.

I patted him on his butt, "Go ahead baby, I'll be in there in a minute."

I knew Lil Carter was probably afraid there would be another argument which would lead to a fight but I thought to myself; *shit...what more damage could C.J. do to me other than killing me at this point?*

C.J. shut the bathroom door and I got a little scared because whenever he tells Lil Carter to go sit down and shuts the door, he is usually about to start an argument and then a fight.

I stood up to brace myself for what was about to happen. I was literally shaking...cold with fear. If anyone had seen me, they would have thought I was standing in a walk-in freezer the way my teeth were chattering.

"Babe, I'm so sorry." C.J. said again.

I was taken by surprise because I didn't expect to hear those words come out of his mouth.

"Look at you! Oh my God. I'm so sorry. You can't go to work...and you can't go to the hospital. They are going to lock me up if you tell them what happened to your face. I can't go to prison... I can't."

He started crying. I couldn't believe the show he was putting on out of desperation.

He got exactly what we he was trying to get AGAIN... my guilt, loyalty and sympathy. C.J. did (somehow) make me believe he was sorry. I don't know how this man managed to do it to me every time...make me feel like I did something wrong...like I was the one to blame. I literally felt like I caused the entire upset and began crying with him. The whole time I was thinking to myself, *Sky you are so stupid. He is a demon. He did this to you. This is not your fault.*

I kept saying that over and over in my head praying that I would eventually absorb those words and believe it for myself.

C.J. reached out for me and pulled me to his chest. "Babe, you have to believe me. I'm so sorry. I promise I'll never hurt you again."

I don't know why I believed him but I did... just as I had done so so so so so many times before. And every time, that little voice in my head kept saying, *damn girl your dumb without even trying to be.*

C.J. and I went into the bedroom and got in the bed.

"Carter," C.J. called.

"Yes dad." Lil Carter came running to our room.

"Go ahead and finish playing your game. Me and your mom are about to take a nap."

"Ok," Lil Carter said with a smile on his face because he knew that his dad and I had made up.

I fell asleep in his arms that morning and was later awakened by a pounding headache, the smell of food being cooked, and the sound of the vacuum running across the floor.

When I sat up in the bed, I could also smell the aroma of pine-sol. I knew C.J. must have cleaned the house because he used my technique. He got that from me...boiling pine-sol in a pot on the stove to make the whole house smell fresh and clean.

I got that method from my aunt; my mom's sister. Her house was always super clean and smelled like fresh pine-sol. When I was a girl, she would boil pine-sol on the stove while she cleaned the house so I did it as I got older and moved into my own house. I even had my friends and C.J.'s mom doing it.

When I got up out the bed, I felt a little dizzy which caused me to stumble up against the wall. C.J. heard the loud thump, turned off the vacuum, and called my name.

"Sky!" I heard him right before everything went completely black.

CHAPTER 4

IT ONLY HURTS WHEN I BLEED

When I woke up, the coldness in the room caused me to shiver. Moments later, I realized where I was. I was in the hospital.

"C.J., what happened to me?" I tried to move my head but something around it prevented any movement.

"Skylar," I heard a deep voice call to me. I figured it was the doctor.

"Doctor, what's wrong with my head?"

"Skylar, I'm Officer Matthews with the Southfield Police Department. Can I ask you a couple of questions about the robbery?"

"...robbery? What Robbery?" I asked. I was confused.

"Ma'am, your boyfriend... one Mr. Carter Jordan brought you in. He said he found you in the house like this when he and your son Carter came home from getting some things from the grocery store."

At first I was confused but I managed to put two and

two together. C.J. didn't want to go to jail so when I passed out, he must have panicked and had no choice but to rush me to the hospital. He then made up a cockamamie story about our apartment being robbed. Lucky for him, it was believable to them because for the past few months or so prior to my trip to the hospital, several of our neighbors' apartments had been broken into.

"Yes, I was taking a shower while waiting on my boys to come back from the grocery store and then I heard a loud noise...like the door being kicked in. When I called out to C.J. several times, I got no response, so I turned off the shower. I was getting ready to step out the shower and something or someone hit me and that's all I remember."

I had to think fast and hope my story was congruent to his. I couldn't believe I was going along with this lie. I wanted, so desperately, to say to the officer, *can you help me please, it was my boyfriend who did this to my face,* but then I looked up C.J. who was staring at me hard through the glass window. I still could barely see him because the eye that wasn't as swollen before I came to the hospital was more swollen now. Failing to be able to see him was probably for the best because although, I foolishly loved him, I hated him for doing what he had done to me.

After finishing the statement with the officer, I was exhausted trying to think of the next lie to tell. When the officer left...in walks C.J. I was beyond upset. I wanted to completely go off on him but I didn't have the energy.

I noticed Lil Carter wasn't with him. "Where is my baby?"

C.J. was staring at me like he saw a ghost. "He is in a room with a police officer and a social worker."

I immediately panicked. "WHAT, WHERE? WHY?"

My mind started running a mile a minute. "Oh My God! They're going to take my baby," I cried.

"What? NO...of course not. I would never let that happen," C.J. whispered while trying to assure me. "I talked to Carter already and I told him what to say. We're fine Sky. No worries."

I couldn't begin to imagine how my baby must have felt. He was probably scared to death because he was forced to lie and go against everything I instilled in him. I had always taught him to be truthful no matter what the circumstances were.

"C.J., this isn't right. We've always taught him not to lie; now everything we've taught him is being thrown out the window as we speak. I don't like this. Our son is being put in a compromising position. This is our mess...not his."

I started crying out of fear and confusion. I didn't know if I wished that Lil Carter told them the truth or not because I didn't want C.J. to go to jail. Then on the other hand, I also didn't want to take the abuse anymore. I was torn...both physically and emotionally exhausted. I wanted to see Lil Carter before I asked for some pain medication that would put me to sleep, so I could just forget everything for just a little while. I really needed that escape.

Just as I was thinking that; in walks Lil Carter with the biggest smile on his face ever.

"Mommy that Policeman gave me five dollars and the lady gave me a toy!"

"Aww, well you know my baby's charming ways does it all the time, I bragged."

After playing and talking with Lil Carter for a while, I asked C.J. to take him to eat and go home so he could take a nap. The poor thing had been up since 7am.

I was going to get some rest until they decide to keep me or discharge me after the results of my CT scan came back. C.J. didn't say a word. Instead, he just nodded his head. I knew his mind was probably all over the place because this was the worst he had ever seen me. C.J. had done this type of thing all the time but not to this magnitude. I knew he was probably afraid that I would leave for good that time.

Throughout the thirteen year time span of our relationship, C.J. had beaten on me most of the time... *and* cheated. I had probably either threatened to leave or left, but it didn't last long. After a phone call or text message, I would easily be drawn back by his charming ways. I guess it was safe to say that Lil Carter had his charm honest.

I pulled the cord hanging alongside my hospital bed for the nurse.

"Hello, Ms. Skylar. What can I get for you?" a voice

said through the speaker.

"I have a lot of pain in my face and neck. Is there something the Doctor can prescribe me... anything?" I asked.

"Yes, I will let him know right now."

"...I would appreciate that very much."

As I waited for the doctor or the nurse to come in with my medication, I couldn't help but to pray to God.

"Lord, I know I'm stupid. I know you've shown me signs that I keep ignoring, but Lord please, please give me peace in my life. Take me out of this situation if that is your will. Lord, I love C.J. I do. It will probably hurt me more to leave than if I stay, but Lord, I'm at your feet asking... begging for guidance. Lord, please lead me...help me."

When I opened my eyes, the nurse was standing in the door waiting as if she didn't want to interrupt my prayer.

"I'm sorry." I said,

"No, don't be. Skylar, I can always wait on God. "

From that, I knew she must have been a church going woman because of the way she said it and her polite demeanor. She looked to be my age or a year or two younger. She was pretty...had very light skin and long hair. You could tell her mom took care of it since her childhood because it was thick and healthy. When she smiled at me, the first thing I noticed was her pretty white teeth. She reminded me of a girl that I caught C.J. cheating on me with...except she was prettier. I couldn't help but notice how beautiful she was...then I started to think maybe if I was as pretty as my nurse, C.J. would love me more and wouldn't dare hit me in my face. This nurse represented all the women he cheated on me with because they were pretty and light skinned like her.

I had a light brown complexion and thought I was pretty most of the time, but when a woman had been beaten down physically, emotionally and mentally the way I had; it was hard to have a healthy self-esteem. I wasn't completely blind. I knew I was a beautiful woman because I heard it all the time, but when the only man that I wanted, loved, and cared about never said it, I would sometimes forget.

♥♥♥♥♥♥♥♥

"Here is a pain medication that I will put into your IV. It's going to make you really drowsy, Skylar," the nurse said as she was injecting the Dilaudid into my IV drip.

About fifteen minutes later, I started to feel like I was floating on a cloud. I felt like I didn't have a care in the world...and at that time, I needed that. Shit! I loved that medication.

As I was drifting in and out of sleep, I looked up at the door and saw the finest...sexiest man that I had ever saw in my life. He was wheeling a little, old lady into my room helping her onto the patient bed next to

mine. We locked eyes and I tried to say *hello*, but off to

sleepy land I went.

CHAPTER 5

MS.LORETTA

When I woke up, everything was a blur. The last thing I remembered was that fine ass man walking into my hospital room. I thought maybe I was dreaming and it was the medication making him look like he was sent directly from heaven. I never imagined calling a man beautiful but for him...I made an exception. This man had to be one of God's angels because I didn't see him anymore. I soon learned that it wasn't a dream because the little old lady he was wheeling in looked over at me from her bed and said, "Hello, child...I'm Loretta."

She reminded me of my grandmother that had passed away a few months earlier. She had beautiful silver/gray hair, and her skin was flawless...the most even shade of brown I had ever seen. She was a little *bity* old thing too...just like my Grannie (who I missed everyday).

♥♥♥♥♥♥♥

"Did that boy do that to your face, child?" she asked.

I was shocked at her bluntness...she came out and asked me that without giving my feelings a second thought.

"You don't have to answer me; I already know he did."

She caught me off guard. Instead of answering her, I was trying to figure out how she might know. I thought maybe the Police Officers or the Doctor's assumed that (despite what lies I had told) and was discussing it and she overheard them.

"Nobody told me that. I can just tell by the way you looked at him when he was here. I saw the fear in your eye. You're scared, disgusted, confused, and in love, or at least what you *think* is love. You young people wear your hearts on your sleeves now a days. You might be fooling others...maybe even fooling yourself, but us old folks can tell everything that you're going through just by looking at you and watching your body language."

I couldn't say a word because she was right on, and the weird thing was my Granny used to say the same words. My Grandmother only tolerated C.J. because of Lil Carter, but she wasn't too fond of him as a boyfriend to me, nor was she fooled by his act. Before she passed, she kept asking for me to come see her. Something kept me from it...something that I could never figure out no matter how much I tried. Deep down inside, I knew what she wanted. She wanted me to leave C.J. because she knew exactly how much pain he caused me over the years and I wouldn't listen to her. I was ashamed of myself for fooling myself and knowingly going against her wishes.

"She doesn't want you with that boy. Leave before he kills you," the old women cautioned.

My eyes got big; this woman said "she" as if she had spoken with someone regarding my circumstances.

"Who is this "she" that you speak of? Who are you talking about?"

I kept repeating it over and over through my tears.

"Ms. Loretta, who are you talking about when you say that "she" doesn't want me with him?"

Shortly afterwards, Ms. Loretta's medication had kicked in and she was fast asleep.

I kept asking her that daunting question, "Who are you talking about?" It was no use. Deep down inside, I knew who "she" was. "She" was my deceased Grandmother.

I cried myself to sleep after the eerie conversation with Ms. Loretta, which was more like a message from my Granny. I couldn't believe God was speaking through Ms. Loretta for my Granny. I knew it was him because Ms. Loretta has never met me before.

When I woke up, that handsome guy was back in our room standing next to Ms. Loretta's bed. When he heard me waking up, he looked up at me, we locked eyes again, and shamefully, I looked away because of the condition of my face looked. Just as his Grandmother had done a few hours before, he also seemed as if he could see right into my soul.

He was about 6ft 1in tall, brown skin complexion, and athletically built. It was obvious that he worked out because of the impressive size of his arms. He had tattoos covering his left arm; it stood out to me because it looked carefully created...nothing like the jailhouse tattoos I often saw. The sleeveless tank top he wore showed how broad his shoulders were. Needless to say, he wasn't too big or too small...he was just right. I could see most of the tattoo that covered his back; it looked like feathers or wings, and a women or some kind of angel. Part of his arm had feathers on it to look like they were flying off the angel or women.

I was so mesmerized that I didn't realize he was saying *hello* until I was snapped out of my day dream by the nurses rushing into the room. He had pressed my emergency nurse button. I must have looked as if I was staring off into space at him, so he thought maybe I was having a seizure or something.

Oh My God, I was so embarrassed.

"I'm sorry," he said and extended his hand, "I'm Dre'. I thought something was wrong because you wouldn't say anything."

"No, I'm sorry. I was lost in thought."

We both laughed which prompted my face to instantly start hurting again. My laugher ended shortly thereafter.

"Are you ok?" he said with a concerned look on his face.

"Yes, I'm fine; it only hurts when I laugh (trying to mix humor with embarrassment.) It's nice to meet you Dre'. I'm Sky... Skylar."

We shook hands. His hand shake was very firm...not too tight; just tight enough to get my attention.

"That's a pretty name, Sky. I bet you're just as beautiful as your name...underneath all those bruise."

When he said that, I remembered what I was in the hospital for and quickly covered my face. Dre' came closer to my bed and moved my hand away from my face. Quite naturally, I flinched as if he was going to hit me. I knew he wasn't but I guess that is a learned behavior considering the circumstances.

"Skylar," he put up his hands, "I don't put my hands on women. A real man never does that."

"I apologize. I'm so sorry. I just..." I said and he cut me off.

"It's ok... I understand. While you were sleeping, my Grandmother told me what happen to you... well, I kind of pried it out of her. It wasn't hard to do after they gave her that medication," he smiled.

I thought to myself, WOW! This man is fine, his teeth are straight, pearly white, and he had all of them. His dimples made him even more attractive. Lord help me.

"She normally wouldn't reveal people's secrets, but considering she was under the influence." he joked.

We both laughed because I knew exactly what he

meant. That was an icebreaker to distract me from otherwise being embarrassed in that moment.

Ms. Loretta had gotten the same medication they gave me and it would have you spilling your guts. I wished they had given it to me right before the police officer came in to speak with me. I would've told him everything... anything to get me out of that situation.

"Do you need me to handle that for you?" Dre' asked.

I looked up at him in a state of confusion; baffled by his question. "Handle...?"

Before I could fully address the question, Lil Carter and C.J. walked into the room. C.J. saw Dre' standing next to my bed; I knew that facial expression all too well. C.J. was ready to do his favorite thing; which meant he was ready to fight.

"Can I help you, my nigga?" C.J. confronted him.

"Nah." responded Dre." He didn't seem moved by C.J. He was getting ready to say something else to C.J. but I immediately cut him off to calm the brewing discomfort in the room.

"C.J. babe, this is Dre.' He is here with his lovely grandmother in the next bed." I pointed toward Ms. Loretta who was still fast asleep.

As my nervousness began to show, I continued to explain.

"He was just helping me because I couldn't see where the call button was to alert the nurse."

I wanted desperately to maintain the minimal calm I was able to present as I slid the remote connected to my bed, underneath my cover. The other button was on the back of the wall behind the bed, so I knew C.J. would believe me with my eyes being swollen and all. I gave a sigh of relief because I knew what result could come from all this.

"Thank you so much Dre.' It was really nice to meet you."

I extended my hand towards him. When Dre' shook it; he squeezed it. I looked up at him...those eyes of his seemed to look straight into my soul. I was afraid of what he might have seen in me. Dre' already knew I was in an abusive relationship *but was he looking directly at my poor self-image? Could he see the fear? Could he see how C.J. controlled me like a puppet master? Could he see how discouraged I was? Could he see that I needed saving?*

I knew C.J. noticed the looks that were exchanged between Dre' and I. I also knew that he arrogantly ignored it. C.J. enjoyed that he ripped my dreams to shreds and had destroyed my self-esteem enough so he was sure that I couldn't get a *nigga* that looked like Dre' to even notice me or care if I was dead or alive.

I assumed that Dre' was either a drug dealer, or the CEO of a prominent business because he was wearing a watch that looked like it cost more than anything I owned in my entire life. *Dre' was very clean and polished... not like the kind of "clean" of a drug dealer...at least not the kind of gangsters I had grown up around. It was soooo much deeper than that.*

He smelled like a bed of fresh flowers and linen mixed with a splash of cashmere. I was a sucker for a man that smelled good. C.J. didn't care as much about those things. He considered himself clean after a basic shower and shave.

I also noticed the key to his car. It was actually a key fob. I was impressed with the modern technology. According to the emblem on it, I knew it was at least a 2015 BMW. A part of me was envious because I knew what I had at home.

♥♥♥♥♥♥♥♥

The nurse came in and closed the curtain that separated the two beds. Before it completely closed, Dre' and I locked eyes for the last time. C.J watched as the nurse removed the IV needles from the back of my hand. He couldn't even look me in the eyes because he was coward and deep down inside, he knew that his actions made him appear like less of a man to the people who were conscious of his actions; Dre' being one of them. I tried to get him to look at me by staring at him but he wouldn't keep eye contact. I knew he was ashamed of what he did but I also knew it would happen again and next time it might be worse.

CHAPTER 6

CRIMES OF PASSION

A few weeks had passed since my trip to the hospital. Surprisingly, my face and some of the bruises had healed up. There were quite a few fading spots underneath my eyes that reminded me of the black eye my face wore. Self consciously, I wished that the bruises didn't heal so fast. I admit that it was an insane thought, but at least that way, if I already looked beaten up, I was sure that C.J. wouldn't hit me again.

My spirits were broken, and so was my thinking. I had even more peculiar thoughts and it shamed me to believe that he could go back to being my *knight in shining amour.*

Every time he violated me, he was the nicest man ever...an ideal boyfriend. After the beatings, he would clean, cook, and be this wonderfully charming person. He even stayed home more. All of these actions caused me to cast my pain aside and return to *love.*

Sometimes, I was sure that something was wrong with me to think that way, but as bad as I know I shouldn't have...I loved C.J. to death.

For a while, I felt like he had some type of voodoo spell on me. After we got into a fight, all he had to do was wipe away my tears, hug me, and promise me he will never do it again for me to fall back under his spell. Usually, I wasn't superstitious and didn't believe in spells but in my many attempts to make sense of the mental madness hell I was living it...I thought perhaps it could be the case. It was deeper than *stepping on a crack and breaking your momma's back*.

I had heard about the spell used to keep a person in love. Some said to write the person's name down on a slip of paper, pray over it, and place in the freezer and BOOM! That person is bound to you for life.

I checked the freezer every time I broke down and took him back...but nothing.

I'd compare it to when a mother whoops her child for disobeying her, then after the whooping, the child is glued to his/her mother trying to do anything and everything to get her approval. That child never falls out of love with their mother. I use to feel like that all the time when my mom whooped me and I could never understand it. That's called unconditional love...that's what I thought I had for C.J.

CHAPTER 7

THE CLIENT

I was exhausted because I had been working all day at what started off as a part time job on the side. The work was something I found to be somewhat therapeutic. Cleaning houses and organizing them turned into a full time job thanks to friends and family. I was getting referrals left and right.

I was on my way to a consultation for a new home cleaning job. The women I spoke with informed me that it would potentially be a full time contract because her grandmother was very ill and had been in a rehabilitation center. She said she needed help getting her house together for her return home and needed someone to come over and do basic cleaning and laundry. That someone would be me.

The house was located in Bloomfield Township, so I knew they had to have a little money to live out there. All the houses were big.

When I pulled up to the house, I was stunned. It was huge and beautiful. I was thinking that, based on the size, I knew it could probably be a great paying job. Lord knows we need the money.

With C.J. being laid off, I'd been busting my ass trying to make ends meet. As soon as I would get caught up, something would knock me ten steps back.

I pulled into a circular driveway and noticed the two cars that were parked there. The 2015 Cadillac CTS caught my eye then I immediately notice a 2015 BMW i8. My little Pontiac G6 looked like a bucket next to them. I got out and walked up to the huge door and stood there for a few seconds searching for a doorbell but in the spot where a doorbell would typically be was a mini iPad type screen. I pressed the red button on it, and then my face popped up on the screen of the little device. I looked up to see if there was a camera above me. There was one facing me and another one above it that moved around. It seemed to be scanning the premises. Immediately afterwards, a woman popped up on the screen, "How can I help you?"

"Yes...hello, my name is Skylar McDaniel and I'm here for the cleaning consultation."

The huge door opened and greeting me was a beautiful woman that looked strangely familiar. I couldn't quite place where we may have met.

"Hello Skylar, I'm Dre'a... Loretta's granddaughter. This is..." I turned around to see who was walking into the room. I must have looked like I saw a ghost because Dre'a immediately stopped talking and looked at me. I finished what she was going to say... "Dre,' right?"

"Yes, do you two know each other?"

I looked up at Dre' and he was just as I remembered. I found comfort in watching those smiling eyes looking down at me.

"Yes," I answered. "Dre' may not recognize me because when we met, I had been in an accident so I didn't look like myself...with the swelling, and bruises and all."

"Sky? WOW! It's a small world." Dre' said.

 "Yes! Yes! It is! Dre'a, it should've clicked when you mentioned Ms. Loretta's name... and you and Dre' are..."

"...twins." they said in unison; then the both of them smiled.

"Well brother, if you don't mind... show Sky around and let her know what we need. It's very nice meeting you and I hope this is the beginning of a great business relationship," Dre'a said while extending her hand.

"I hope so," I responded. We shook hands and she walked out of the foyer.

The room fell silent as Dre' walked around me as if he was *checking me out.* This unexpected reaction made me feel very uncomfortable.

"So I was right?" he asked.

 I looked at him confused. "Right about what?".

"You are even more beautiful under all those bruises."

I couldn't resist smiling slightly trying not to let him see me blush; it was difficult.

"Thank you... I guess."

"What do you mean by *you guess*? Don't tell me that you don't think you're beautiful."

He looked me straight in the eyes while talking to me, and that also made me feel uncomfortable and weird, but at the same time...desirable. I wasn't sure what or how to feel. This man had me thinking naughty sexual thoughts about him and it left me wondering if he could see right through me. *Who are you?*

"I mean... I think I'm ok. I wouldn't say I'm beautiful. My idea of *beautiful* is Halle Berry, Nia Long, and Stacey Dash. I can't compare myself anywhere near them."

Dre' moved closer to me...so close that I could smell his cologne. He was wearing the same fragrance as when we first met at the hospital. I was intoxicated and hypnotized by the scent as I inhaled it so that I could take in all of him.

"Those women can't light a match to you. You are naturally beautiful, with no surgery, and no makeup... nothing... just beauty."

I didn't know what it was about that man, but I was like high off his presence. I had never felt like that. I had never even looked at another man the whole thirteen years of my relationship with C.J.

I needed to snap out of it but I couldn't. My mind was

racing with thoughts of him.

Dre' moved closer to me. When I tried to move back, I bumped up against the wall of a walk-in closet door that was open, so I continued to move back into the closet to escape him. Dre' followed me all the while; looking me directly into my eyes as if he could see into my soul. Those bright eyes may have looked cold and scary to the average person, but they seemed warm and loving to me.

"Excuse me...umm, what are you doing?" I asked, through my shaking voice.

I don't know if I was scared or turned on, but I knew for certain that whatever spiritual possession he had put on me definitely had me sexually high and dying from curiosity.

The space between my legs was moist, hot and throbbing with passion. I'd never felt like that for another man since I had been with C.J. It had been so long that the experience felt brand new...and I liked the refresher's course in what I was about to learn.

"I want you Sky. Can I have you?"

"Huh? Umm...I don't think so. This is supposed to be a business meeting."

Those were the words I was saying, but in my head I was thinking, *yes Dre,' yes.*

Dre' was so sexy in every way imaginable. His eyes, lips and arms alone, were making me about to have an orgasm.

The next thing I knew, he closed the door to the closet we were in and locked it. We were in the dark with just the red light from the camera on the ceiling which gave off enough light so that we could see each other, but it was still dark. I felt like a scared mouse backed up into a corner by a big brown cat and it was turning me on. Again, I tried desperately to snap out of it but I was in a sexual high and the momentum was building. The very thought of the camera recording us turned me on...and I got hotter and hotter and wanted Dre' to take and do whatever he wanted with me.

Dre' reached out for me and pulled me close to him, grabbed my neck, and pushed my face up toward him with his thumb. He had a very slight grip around my neck and face. His hands were big, but he didn't move or grip my neck the way C.J. would grip my neck. It was more sensual and sexual. When he kissed my lips, I closed my eyes and waited on the next one. We kissed like we were in love. Our bodies were so in tune that before I knew it, my panties were soaking wet.

I had on a dress. Prior to coming to the house, I had gone home to change and freshen up because I had this...well... what was supposed to be a business consultation which had turned into anything but.

Dre' took his shirt off and judging by the glare of the red light from the camera, I could see his chest and his wash board stomach.

I felt as if I was going to explode. I was beyond horny at that point.

I was up against the wall which made it easier for Dre'

to pull my dress up, grab my ass, and picked me up. He sat me on top of a tall dresser in the closet so my pussy was eye level to him.

I couldn't believe I was going through with it. Typically, that wasn't like me. I thought I must have been having one of those *wet dreams* and I needed to pinch myself so I could wake up because if I was moaning in my sleep, C.J. was not going to like that and would definitely start a fight. I could hear him hollering, "Who the fuck were you dreaming about? It sounds like you were fucking to me."

I quickly realized it wasn't a dream after I felt Dre's warm tongue run over my panties. I wanted to scream, *"Take them off... PLEASE TAKE THEM OFF!"*

He took both hands and ripped my panties apart with one try. My pussy was greeting him right at eye level, like *"Hello, Daddy."*

Dre' took both hands and wrapped them around my waist to sort of pull my pelvis towards him...and he immediately went to work.

First, he kissed me like he was making love to me with his mouth and tongue. I couldn't resist or hold back...I came so hard that my body was convulsing like I was having a seizure. He moved to the side for only a second because I squirted all the way across the room. I had never felt that before... my body continued shaking uncontrollably with gratitude.

He started again...I tried, with all my strength, to move away from him, but he took his arm and put it around my waist. He was holding me down tight and I was turned on by the way he controlled me.

The feeling was rising in between my legs again and before I knew it, I screamed so loud you would've thought the neighbors heard me. It seemed we both totally forgot that his sister was still there in the house... at least I did, but what I didn't know was that the closet was sound proof. I would find that out later.

After he was done, I couldn't move. I was stuck in that position. He picked me up to get me down from the dresser. I looked up at Dre' when he put me down to see that he was licking the remainder of my juices from his lips.

He grabbed my face and asked, "Do you want to see what you taste like?" and kissed me so hard my pussy started throbbing again.

He had on gray jogging pants and his dick was rock hard...so hard that I could see it lying on his leg. My eyes nearly popped out of my head. I became instantly afraid. Dre' caught me looking so he grabbed it and *hmm*, it was so thick.

"You want me, or are you scared?"

I looked him in his eyes like he would do to me to show him I was being honest.

"I'm scared."

"Skylar, don't be; I'll take it slow," he whispered.

We kissed and again, he made me high off his lust for

me. All I kept thinking was, *I hope C.J. doesn't try to get some tonight.*

Dre' was working with about ten inches and it was going to take a lot of Kegel exercises to get back ready for C.J.'s mediocre six and a half inches.

I watched Dre' as he pulled his penis out and held it in his hand. It was the prettiest site I'd ever seen. The skin on it was smooth.

He motioned for me to come closer to him and I did. Dre' kissed me passionately again and I could feel that sweet, tingling sensation between my legs. It was so thick that I could barely wrap my hand around it. He massaged my clit all the while looking me right in the eyes...and used his free hand to hold his dick.

"Do you want me to stop, Sky?"

My mind and conscious wanted to say, *"Yes, please stop. I'm not supposed to be doing this,"* but my body had taken over saying. *"Hell no! Don't stop,"*

I nodded my head *yes* then *no.* he knew I wanted his fine ass so badly so he didn't stop. Needless to say, my body won the emotional fight.

"Come here," he said while motioning for me to get on my knees. As he leaned against the wall to brace himself, I knew exactly what he wanted and I obeyed his request. I couldn't believe that this man that I only met once and knew nothing of had me being submissive. I was a lot of things but submissive I wasn't. I liked the feeling of his control. Although you would think that because of C.J., I would run away from a man that was trying to control me, but C.J.'s control was *mental and physical abusive* control that tore me down. With Dre,' it was *sexual, mind and body* control... and it felt good. I wanted more.

I got down on my knees and looked up at him, pleading with my eyes. "Please don't hurt me."

He smiled and in his mind he said, "I won't babe."

I took him in my mouth slowly at first because it was so big. Once my mouth was completely wet, I went to work. It was turning me on to be turning him on. I could hear his moans and feel his legs wanting to give out on him, as they were shaking. Five minutes hadn't even passed before Dre' pulled back.

I stayed in that exact position with my mouth wide open. Once he realized it, he smiled again and put it back in my mouth.

Normally after finishing on some head like that, a man's dick would go limp and he needs a minute, but not Dre.' I think it was harder at that point than before.

He lifted me up off my knees and picked me up. I was shaking with nervous anticipation because I didn't know how bad it would hurt going in but I knew I wanted it....hungered for it. We both paused and looked at each other and in unison we said, "*Condom!*" Dre' reached at the top of one of the shelves we were standing next to and grabbed it and gave the condom to me.

"Open it for me," he coached.

I noticed that the gold and black Magnum package had big, bold print letters that read *XXXL*. My heart started beating fast as hell...I guess the look of concern showed on my face.

Dre' smiled and said, "I promise I won't hurt you. Sky, if you want me to stop, I will."

Like an innocent girl I responded, "Ok."

For some odd reason, I trusted him.

Dre' was still holding me with my legs wrapped around his waist. I couldn't help but to think about how strong he was because I wasn't exactly a small girl. I weighed one hundred and eighty pounds and stood five feet and ten inches tall.

Dre' kissed me like he loved me which prompted the throbbing to start again. Next, he walked over to the ottoman that was in the middle of the floor in the closet and laid me back on it. When I sat up, he pulled my dress over my head to completely remove it, then he unfastened my bra...it fell off. Dre' stood back and admired my completely naked body. I was even more self-conscious in front of Dre' than I usually was. While it was true that my friends always told me my body was amazing, I didn't think so. C.J. ridiculed me by calling me fat at any give opportunity, so needless to say, my self-esteem wasn't exactly the highest.

"Sky, you are beautiful."

 "Thank you," I said blushing.

I removed my hand from around my waist uncovering

myself. Dre' made me feel as if I was as beautiful as he said I was.

He kneeled down on top of me between my legs, I was so nervous and scared... like I was a virgin having sex for the first time.

I was *so* far from being a virgin but I might as well have been because I had sex with the same man for thirteen years.

He kissed my thighs all the way down to my feet and back up to my lips without missing an inch of my body. With Dre,' I felt superior...like I was the only women he wanted in the world.

He didn't have to guide his dick in. It belonged there and it was evident by the way it slid right in. It was absolutely perfect...I fit like a really tight glove around it.

I gasped at the first stroke, as it was a mixture of pain and pleasure. He moved in and out slowly. My pussy was so wet that it was making all kinds of crazy noises. I don't think I'd ever been that wet and horny before in my life.

Dre' leaned up without missing a beat, licked his fingers, and placed them on my clit rubbing it soft then hard. It was driving me crazy...so crazy I could feel myself about to cum.

"Let it out babe. Don't be scared. You gonna make me love this pussy, Sky."

The sound of his voice talking shit mixed with his dick

and hand rubbing on my clit wouldn't allow me to hold it in anymore. I came so hard I could feel the tears rolling down my face. My pussy was still throbbing; yet I still wanted more. Dre' started stroking faster and then grabbed my hips.

I was never the type of girl that made love. It wasn't that I didn't like to make love...I most enjoyed rough sex and love making only from *time to time*. I felt he could read my mind because not even a second after that thought crossed my mind, he was fucking the shit outta me. I was screaming and moaning so loud that my voice started to get horse.

"Yes Dre' babe, fuck me!" I screamed

"Sky, I couldn't stop thinking about you after you left the hospital that day. I want to love you, protect you, take care of you, and make love to you."

"I won't ever hurt you Skylar, can I? Will you let me do that?" he said through strokes.

My emotions were in over drive.

My mind and heart was at war again. My mind was saying, "Yes Dre!' Keep fucking me like this and you can have whatever you want from me."

My heart, on the other hand was saying, "No Sky! You have a man at home...surely you remember him; C.J... your son's father?"

C.J. would never let me leave without a fight. He would probably kill before he let another man, especially someone like Dre,' have me. I was baffled as I was thinking, *but isn't this the life I've longed for with happiness, a man that loves me and would never hurt me, mentally, physically or emotionally? I deserved to be treated like a queen and have a man all to myself...not having to share him with anyone else. I was worthy of having someone who could see through to my soul like Dre's eyes seemed to do.*

I wanted that so bad, but I knew the moment I left Dre' that day, I would be home and slapped in the face by reality LITERALLY!!

Both Dre' and I were reaching our climax at the same time. It was almost like it was meant to be. It was so delicious that tears were rolling down my face. I wanted it to last forever, but I knew I would never be able to get away from C.J.

I started crying silently because I wanted happiness, and at that moment, I knew Dre' could give that to me.

Dre' compassionately wiped the tears from my eyes.

"Sky, I can always take care of that for you. All you have to do is give me the word."

I couldn't believe that Dre' was asking me that again. I tried to play dumb when he asked me this before at the hospital, but I knew exactly what he meant. I wondered this. *What kind of person was he to be able to kill so easily for someone like me...someone that he hardly knew?*

"Dre,' I know what you want me to say, but it's not that easy. We have a son and I have a conscious."

I sighed, because deep down I had a strange feeling that Dre' may have made up his mind to do this before he asked me. Those eyes of his were cold and dark, but at the same time, loving and warm. I was too scared to ask him what he did for a living. I thought I would rather not know as that would probably be safer. At that moment, I got scared and tried to stay calm so that Dre' wouldn't notice. I was thinking that I may have just sold my soul to the devil.

Dre' lead me to the bathroom. Once I was in there, I couldn't believe my eyes. The room was like something out of a movie. This bathroom was huge and breathtaking. I fell in love with the bath tub centered in the floor like in the Scarface movie. There was walk-in shower with shower heads on each wall.

"This is your grandmother's house right?" I asked,

I couldn't believe someone her age would have a bathroom like this. Dre' seemed amused at the look on my face so much so that he laughed.

"...yeah, but this one is my private bathroom for when I stay over at the house. This is light... you should see her bathroom."

I couldn't believe it. The bathroom in my apartment looked like a portable potty compared to it.

"Would you like to take a hot bath or a shower?"

"...a shower would be best because I have to get going."

Truth be told, at that moment, I wanted to grab my

clothes and haul ass out of there and never look back! I was terribly ashamed of what I had just done, but it was something about Dre's aura and his presence that sparked my curiosity. I wanted to know more about him. I wanted him to make me love him, and I wanted to make him love me.

Dre' lead me over to the shower and turned on the water. When he did that, Trey Songz "Sex Ain't Better Than Love" was blaring through the speakers in the ceiling.

I smiled because I knew that he had no idea that Trey Songz was my favorite artist.

"Go ahead," he motioned toward the shower, "I'll be right back. I have to make a phone call."

As I stepped in the shower, my mind started to wonder; could I have all this if I take Dre' up on his offer?

I couldn't believe I was considering it, but so many times I had wished death upon C.J. after he beat me unconscious. It was a pattern I had... once the bruises healed, so would my heart.

The whole thing was crazy. I often wondered if he damaged something considering all the times he hit me in the head.

My emotions were taking over so I began to cry uncontrollably. I did the best thing that I knew to do; I fell to my knees in prayer; "Lord, what's happening to me? This couldn't be your plan for my life. Help me to escape this hell and torment."

Dre' stepped into the shower, picked me up, and held me in his arms. "No more hurt...No more pain. I got you."

I felt so safe in his arms.

After showering, I got dressed. My hair was completely a mess, so I wet it and pulled it up in a ponytail. Thank God it was raining really badly outside. I could blame my hair being messed up on that. I knew C.J. would ask because I had just gotten my hair done the day before.

Dre' and I walked to the door and he looked down at me. I had my head down because I was still a little ashamed of what we had just done. Dre' lifted my chin with his finger.

"I got you Sky. No more worries and no more fear."

He kissed me on my forehead before I turned to walk out of the door, then he grabbed my hand, "I have something for you".

He handed me a check that he wrote out to me for twenty thousand dollars. I was speechless and the shocked look must have shown on my face. It soon dawned on me... *is he trying to pay me for sex?*

"...For your cleaning services in advance. I would still love for you to assist us in getting my grandmother's house ready for when she comes home." he confirmed.

"...Yes, um, yes, but my services won't cost this much." I was growing increasingly confused.

"I know that," he clarified. "The extra nineteen thousand dollars is a tip." He then kissed me on the forehead just one more time before I left.

I smiled, "Thank you. This is really kind of you." then I walked out to my car.

I could feel Dre's eyes watching me the whole time so I didn't turn around to wave *good-bye* until I made it to the car.

I started the car up and drove away. Shortly afterwards, I pulled into a gas station a few miles down the road. I didn't need any gas. I needed to gather my thoughts. I put my head down into my hands. I couldn't believe what I had just done. *I didn't even know this man.* I prayed out loud, or should I say, I repented? *"Lord please forgive me for this."*

I reached over into the passenger's seat, grabbed the check that Dre' handed me, and I looked at it again... Twenty Thousand dollars? Wow! I really needed this money. *I would be able to get caught up on so many bills and even pay my car loan off.* I was excited at the thought.

I began to cry because I didn't know if it was ok to be happy, sad or scared; I just didn't know. I had never cheated on C.J. before and I felt the lowest of the low, but then again I thought, *ooh so what Sky, you had amazing sex with this handsome sexy ass man. C.J. cheats on you damn near every day.*

It was like I had the little good angel on my right, telling me to be a good women, give the check back to

Dre,' and cut all ties with him.

On the flip side, the little devil on my left shoulder was saying *girl fuck C.J. he doesn't want to see you succeed, he thinks he owns you. He thinks you fear him all he will do is continue to destroy you mentally, physically and emotionally.*

I was so emotionally overwhelmed that I sat in my car at that gas station for about thirty minutes and cried. I knew I needed to get it together before I went home.

CHAPTER 8

ASK ME NO QUESTIONS

When I pulled up to my apartment, I checked myself in the mirror. My face was a little red but it was a good thing that it was raining outside because I could blame it on my allergies in case C.J. asked any questions.

I could hear him talking as I was walking up to the door. C.J. must have been sitting on the couch on the phone because I couldn't hear anyone else talking. He wasn't even trying to be discreet.

"Babe, I'll be leaving as soon as Sky gets home. I can't just leave my son here. So... you gonna have that pussy ready and wet for me when I get there?"

I couldn't believe how loudly he was talking. C.J. didn't care if I walked up or walked in on his conversations. That behavior and lack of respect was nothing new to me. Although I was conscious of it, that didn't soften the blow of it. C.J.'s phone has dialed my number by mistake plenty of times. He would sometimes be in the middle of lying to a bitch about being single, arguing with a bitch, and on a few occasions, fucking a bitch. Whatever the case was, I could hear everything.

Although I was super upset, I had learned how to pick and chose my battles with him because I never came out the one right. At the times that I was right, I was still wrong according to C.J.'s logic (or lack thereof). The sad conclusion of it all was that I would still end up with a black eye and bruises and scratches everywhere.

The thought of the entire situation pissed me off because there I was regretting what happened earlier that day with Dre' and was thinking about how I could make our lives better with the twenty thousand dollar check I received from Dre'.

It was always difficult for me to conceal my feelings when I was angry. Anyone looking at me could always see the emotions written all over my face and I hated that about myself.

♥♥♥♥♥♥♥

As I put my key in the door and opened it, C.J. was hanging up the call. The look on my face must have told him I was outside the door and heard his conversation. Quite naturally, he would be irrational in his reaction.

"Fuck you looking like that for?" he asked.

I didn't say anything. Instead, I just took off my shoes and headed to our bedroom in sheer disgust.

"Bitch, I don't know why you mad. If you do what the

fuck a women is supposed to do for her man then I wouldn't have to be fucking or getting my dick sucked by no other bitches!"

Unfortunately, I knew exactly where this was going. Even when I said nothing, he would still make it out to be an issue.

I could hear him walking toward the room, so I braced myself. This was typical of C.J. Whenever he was caught in his web of lies and deception, he would attempt to use reverse psychology on me and make it out to be about my faults in our relationship. The conclusion of such a heated debate would always end with him hitting me.

"You know what I don't understand? I don't understand how you walk in the house with an attitude everyday!" He said this while standing in the door way with his arms folded.

"I don't have an attitude everyday...even considering that I walked up on your conversation, talking to another random bitch about having her pussy ready for when you got there," I said shaking my head.

I couldn't believe he had the audacity to try to argue with me over what he had just done, but that was nothing new to me; it happened all the time. Most of the time, I kept my mouth shut, but other times like *this* time, I couldn't. It was too much disrespect and anger wouldn't allow the silence.

"Bitch, do what the fuck you're supposed to do as a

woman and I wouldn't have to get it in the street!" he screamed.

I rolled my eyes in disgust and he saw it. The next thing I knew, he swung and hit me in the side of my face with the back of his hand. It stung so bad I couldn't hold back the urge to cry. As much as I didn't want to let him see me cry, I simply couldn't help it.

With a face full of tears, I pitifully asked, "C.J., why did you hit me? I didn't even say anything."

"I did it because I'm sick of your bitch ass! You want to come in here with an attitude and rolling your fucking eyes. Bitch, roll them again!" he warned.

As he said that, he lunged across the bed at me and grabbed my hair, which caused my neck to jerk back, I heard something pop. The pain was excruciating. Shortly afterwards, I grew dizzy. I laid on the floor in a ball trying to cover up my face, but C.J. grabbed my arms and twisted them. He hit me in my face several times with his free hand. Finally, he stopped when my nose started to bleed and walked out of the room,

"I'm not fucking with you no more! I'm leaving!"

He used this incident as an opportunity to do what he wanted to do.

That was also pretty typical of him. It was obvious that whoever that girl was that he was talking on the phone with before I came in, must have wanted him to spend the night with her. In order to not feel guilty about his deceitful antics, he starts a fight with me so he can use that as an excuse to not come home. It was perfect timing!

Still lying on the floor crying silently, I wished he would stay gone that time (as with many times). I was really getting sick of it....full to brim with nonsense.

I waited in the bedroom until I knew for sure he was gone and then I picked up the phone and held it. I wanted to dial 911 so badly, but I couldn't. I cried louder because I knew; in fact, I was sure that was all I needed to do, but I couldn't put Lil Carter through that. Risking that was unheard. Honestly, I needed our son just as much as he needed me.

I started thinking about who I could call. Sadly, I was fully aware that I didn't have anyone I could talk to without them judging me. I was blessed to have lots of family but they all hated C.J. with good reason. I didn't want to hear the "*I told you so (s)*" from them at such a delicate time. I already felt horrible and their comments would only confirm how stupid I felt for loving and continuing on with him.

I cried so hard that I felt I couldn't breathe.

In these moments, I wished that I could call my mom. She was the one person who would give me the encouragement that I needed in the midst of it all. She would tell me to pack my things and come to her house...never burdening me with all the extra stuff that I would have to hear from other family members.

Unfortunately, she was not there anymore. She passed away six months earlier from kidney failure. I had been dealing with depression ever since and it was getting worse because of things that I was going through with C.J.

I spoke out loud to God, "Lord, why are you punishing me? What have I done to deserve this? First the abuse ...then my mom. Why Lord?"

I didn't want to blame or resent God, but I couldn't understand the pain I was going through.

I had to get myself together before Lil Carter came in the house, so I got off the floor and headed to the bathroom to fix my hair, wipe away the blood from my nose, and wash my face. When I looked in the mirror, I saw red marks all over my face and my lips. There was swelling underneath my eye and the bruises had already begun to form.

After washing my face, I tried to conceal the trouble spots with the makeup. It really wasn't working, but I thought it would work well enough to where our son wouldn't notice.

My neck and arm was hurting so badly that I took two Vicodin pills that C.J. had in the closet. He kept those kinds of pain pills because he would sell them from time to time. I had no idea where he was getting them from.

After a while, I started to feel better. Those pills had me happy and feeling as if I was floating on a cloud. They did exactly what they were supposed to do... make me forget about everything that happened.

I liked the feeling they gave me so I went back into the

closet and poured more pills in my hand to hide for the next time I needed them. Sadly, I was sure he would take his anger out on me. There were over three hundred pills so I knew C.J. wouldn't notice some missing.

I sat back and listened to some music. The effects of the pills caused my mind to wander off. I became consumed with thoughts about the things I had done earlier that day with Dre.' I couldn't help but smile at how spontaneous I was with him. I normally wouldn't dare do stuff like that, but to be honest I loved it. I loved the way Dre' made me feel. I thought to myself since C.J. won't be back tonight... *I should find a sitter for Lil Carter and go see him.* Reality set in after I realized all the bruises on my face. I quickly changed my mind.

It was like Dre' knew I was thinking of him because at that very moment, I got a text to my phone from a number I didn't recognize. It read:

Sky, this is Dre.' I want you now! Meet me in two hours at 23812 Chestnut Circle in Southfield.

The biggest smile came across my face. I couldn't believe he was still thinking about me. I contemplated texting him back then finally I said *fuck it, I'll put on just enough makeup to cover up the bruises.*

I showered and oiled up, got dressed and made sure I put on my favorite perfume...the fragrance that everyone always complimented me on. I finished curling my hair and fixed it so that my side ban would fall over the bruised eye. Afterwards, I applied makeup which I never wore...in fact, I bought for days like those...when C.J. would attack me and I might need to cover up his signatures before going out into the public.

I picked out a super cute sun dress because it was really warm outside.

I texted my cousin to see if she could watch Lil Carter for a while and then I went outside to look for him. He was never far away. We lived in an apartment complex where everybody knew everybody.

After I dropped Lil Carter off, my nerves were starting to get the best of me. I sat in the car in front of my cousin's house having second thoughts. *This is not right. I shouldn't be doing this.* Then I thought about what C.J. was probably doing during my moment of indecisiveness so I decided to go through with it. I drove to meet Dre'.

CHAPTER 9

DRE' DAY

I pulled up unsure of which condo was Dre's' because they all looked similar so I checked my text messages to look at the address. There was a Range Rover parked out front, but I still wasn't sure if it was the correct house because I didn't see either of the cars that were parked outside Ms. Loretta's house. When I parked and got out, Dre' was standing in the doorway anticipating my arrival.

I smiled, "Hello."

"Hello gorgeous," Dre' greeted me.

He looked better than he had when I saw him earlier. Looking at him made me want him more and more. I longed for his kiss, his touch, his taste...all of him all over me.

"I ordered some dinner. You haven't eaten yet, have you?"

"No, I haven't."

"It's J. Alexander's steak and potatoes. Is that ok?"

"Yes, that's perfect. I haven't eaten all day...I'm famished."

When I stepped inside the condo, I was in awe at its beauty. It was amazing. In the foyer, there was dark grey wood floors and dark grey plush carpet in the livening room that lead up the stairs. The furniture was extravagant. The air in the house smelled of vanilla. There was a huge flat screen seventy inch television mounted to the wall playing soft jazz music. There was a patio door that was open which allowed me to see outside. The back patio faced a huge pond. The patio table was set with our food, wine, and chocolate covered strawberries (one of my favorite desserts). The view and ambiance was inviting and relaxing. Temporarily, my nerves were no longer on edge. I felt like I was on vacation from all the bullshit that was going on in my life and it felt damn good.

Dre' was returning from the patio with a bottle of Earl Stevens Mango Mascoto in his hand with two wine glasses. He handed me a glass and poured me some wine. I inhaled the fruity, citrusy smell from the wine and it smelled and tasted delicious.

Dre' lead me out to the patio. I could still hear the music playing through the speakers mounted on the concrete walls of the patio. Dre' noticed me admiring the speakers.

"Would you like me to put on some other kind of music?"

"No this is good. I've never listened to jazz but I like it; it's really relaxing."

"Yeah, that's why I listen to it... clears my mind, ya know?"

"Yeah," I smiled.

"You have such a beautiful smile and your teeth are really straight and white. Are they false teeth?" he asked with a smirk on his face.

"No," I said... and we laughed.

We ate and talked and drank almost two bottles of wine. The food was so on point. I was starting to feel a little tipsy. I knew it because I kept nervously smiling every time Dre' would look at me. When he talked to you, he would look you directly in the eyes.

He stopped smiling and was staring at me.

"What's wrong?" I asked.

"Do you have make-up on, Sky?"

He must have started noticing because it was sticky, hot and humid from the rain earlier and my face was sweating.

"Yes, why do you ask?"

"I ask because I can see the bruises that you're trying to cover up under your eye."

The smile faded and looked down at my hands. I was so embarrassed. I knew he must have been thinking I was the dumbest women that he ever met to be letting a man continue to beat on me. It wasn't even a few weeks since he first met me in the hospital, when C.J. had disfigured my face. Tears began to well up in my eyes. I didn't want to look at him so that he wouldn't see that I was ashamed.

"Look at me, Sky."

I looked up and couldn't control the tears that had begun to fall. He got up from his seat and stood me up.

"Listen, I'm not here to judge you. I really like you and I can help you get out of that. Let me help you Sky," he plead.

"It's not that easy Dre.' I could've walked away a long time ago, but the type of person C.J. is... he would continue to make my life a living hell. I've thought about moving out of town... just packing up a little of me and Lil Carter's things and disappear, but what will that do to my son? He won't be able to see or talk to his dad. It's just not that easy Dre'... it's just not."

I began to cry harder. I couldn't believe that I was expressing all this, and telling my secrets to him. Dre' moved closer to me and hugged me. "Come on," he said, and took my hand and lead me to his huge bathroom. He went to the closet and removed a face towel.

"Here, wash your face. You shouldn't ever wear makeup, it's not who you are. You're naturally beautiful and you don't need that."

I washed my face and looked in the mirror. I couldn't see what Dre' saw in me. All I could see was the bruises C.J. gave me. After finishing, I walked into the bedroom that the double door bathroom lead to. Dre' was sitting on the ottoman at the foot of the king sized bed.

"Come here, beautiful."

I walked toward him, and sat between his legs. He leaned back to give me room to put my feet up. I kicked off my sandals before doing so.

"Listen, I don't know why I'm drawn to you, but I am. No man should put his hands on his queen. I'm very sensitive to that because my mom was beaten to death by my father. It happened in front of Dre'a and me. He had been beating on her as long as I can remember. We were only thirteen years old when it happened. My mom would always tell us not to tell anyone and would act as if nothing was wrong... like you are doing Sky. I knew she was dying inside. He had killed her long before that night but she kept a happy face on for me and Dre'a .That night after he beat her to death, I went into their bedroom, got his gun, and shot him in the head...killing him. When the police got there, they thought it was a murder/suicide and my grandmother... my mom's mother (Ms. Loretta), let the police think that was the case so I wouldn't go to jail. We've kept that secret for a long time and I've never told anyone this ever, but I feel like I needed to tell you this to protect you and your son. Don't fool yourself...it will never stop. He will always be that person. People like him and my dad don't change so you have to get out before your son is burying you or both of yall."

What Dre' was saying opened my eyes. It was like an epiphany. I couldn't believe what he was telling me... someone so passionate and so caring had killed before. I guess that's what I saw in those eyes of his... a loving heart turned cold.

Dre' and I sat and talked for what seemed like forever. When I looked up, it was three in the morning.

Oh my God, it's really late. I didn't have my phone. It was in the living room on vibrate so I didn't know if C.J. had called or anything. I jumped up and ran to get my phone. When I looked at my phone, I had ninety missed calls from C.J. and ten voice mails. I thought to myself, *he's going to kill me.*

When Dre' walked into the living room, I was pacing the floor. I was shaking with worry.

"Is everything ok?" he asked.

"C.J. called a bunch of times."

Dre' saw the nervousness on my face.

"Listen, you can stay here if you're scared to go home tonight."

"Ok, I think that's best. I don't want to go get Lil Carter this late and I definitely don't want to go home by myself if C.J.'s there... so I'll stay...thank you."

I picked up my phone and called my cousin to make sure Lil Carter was ok. She reassured me that he was fine and told me that I could come by in the morning. I was relieved that I didn't have to go endure yet another ass whooping on that night.

I followed Dre' back into the bedroom. He handed me one of his long t-shirt to sleep in.

"I can sleep in the guest bedroom if you would like," he said suggested.

I smirked, "Dre,' I think it's a little too late for that. We made..." I stopped myself because I almost said "*we made love.*" I actually wasn't sure if we did. *Did we make love? Was that love making?*" It sure felt like it.

"...had sex, I mean... so I think were acquainted enough to sleep in the same bed."

He laughed and disappeared into the bathroom and then I heard the shower come on. I couldn't believe I was spending the night with another man.

CHAPTER 10

KISSES DON'T LIE

Dre'

What are you doing? This was supposed to be a job and I'm getting way too involved with her. She wasn't supposed to be so willing to let me into her life...this stupid girl.

I was developing feelings for her. I wanted to get her out of the hell she was living in, and protect and take care of her forever. That was the goal here.

Dre,' man you tripping. Just do this job and forget that yall ever met.

I stepped inside the shower and stood underneath the hot running water. The pressure from the flow of the water felt soothing.

I could just take care of that tonight. Nobody knows where she is and that would make it easier to go take care of C.J. What about the little boy? How would I get to him?

I was a professional and never questioned myself when it came to completing a job, but I also never developed feelings for a mark either.

I wiped my face with some water and shook my head. Where were these feelings coming from? I've never loved and I promised myself I never would after losing my mom and being forced to kill my father. I grew up way before I wanted to and it turned my heart cold. In order to protect the only ones I do love and have left (my grandmother and sister), I have to complete this job.

I felt a draft from the shower door opening. When I turned around, the most beautiful site I've ever seen was standing and waiting for me to invite her in. Sky had undressed and wanted to join me in the shower. She had pulled her hair up in a ponytail in the center of her head. Sky was so beautiful. I reached out for her to give me her hand and then she stepped inside the shower. As I looked down at her, I could see the pain and fear in her eyes. She wanted me to rescue her from that hell, but she wasn't going to tell me that. I leaned down to kiss her and it was like she sent me on a sexual high every time I kissed her soft lips. Sky had mastered the art of kissing and I felt her soul belonged to me. I picked her up and she wrapped her legs around me. I knew we were going to make love that night. Although I would never have sex without a condom because hoes can't be trusted, I knew Skylar was different.

My dick knew exactly where to go...like her pussy had suction on it because when I picked her up, it slid right in. We didn't have sex in the shower, but we definitely made love. Her pussy felt soooo good and it fit like a glove around my dick. She was made just for me.

The faces she made when I was stroking it turned me on. She would look me right in the eyes and I could read her mind. Sky wanted all of me and that's exactly what I gave her. We both were yearning each other and at the same time, we climaxed. She came all on my dick and I came all in her pussy. With this being the case, I just complicated this job more, but at that moment I didn't care. Skylar felt so good and for that night, she was all mine. Sky slept in my arms that night and I watched her as she slept. She was sleeping like a baby because she felt she was safe with me. I contemplated what I had to do, but as I lay there with her, I couldn't go through with it. I wanted to protect her from harm not bring it to her.

I fell asleep and was waken in the morning by my cell phone ringing. When I rolled over, I looked at it and it was an unknown number. I knew that could be only one person, so I slid out of bed and went in the living room, and then out onto the patio.

"Hello, Mr. Santiago," I said when I answered the phone.

"Hello, Dre,'" he said, with his heavy accent. "I understand that you have made contact with the girl."

"Yes, I have. My sister hired her to clean my grandmother's home like I instructed her to do."

I didn't want to tell him that I made more than just contact with her and she was asleep in my bed as we speak,

"Mr. Santiago, is it absolutely necessary for me to kill the girl and the kid? Why not just him?"

Mr. Santiago's voice was very stern. "Dre,' I hired you to do a job... not ask questions. He ran off with a large amount of cocaine and pills and I haven't heard from him. Had he called me to explain, I would have spared his bitch's life and his bastard son... but he didn't. Complete the job Dre' or then me and you have a bigger problem."

I heard the dial tone and tried to calm my nerves before going back to bed. When I walked back into the bedroom, Sky was coming out of the bathroom.

"I'm sorry Sky, did I wake you?"

"No, I just had to use the bathroom."

She climbed back into bed. When I climbed in behind her, she was visibly shaking.

"Are you ok?"

I wondered if she had heard the conversation I had with Mr. Santiago on the phone.

"Yes, I'm just cold." She laid back down next to me with her back to me. When I went to put my arm around her, she jumped... and I knew something was wrong. I figured she was still nervous about going home.

"Sky no need to be scared. I would never hurt you."

I wanted to assure her of that.

She wasn't use to a man touching her that wasn't beating her. This all brought back memories…painful ones. I remember my mom always being the same way… really jumpy and jittery.

CHAPTER 11

LYING KISSES

Sky

Little did he know I had gone to the bathroom when I heard him get up and answer his phone. Dre' had an intercom system that was hooked up to every room in the condo; including the outside patio. I pressed the *listen* button to the intercom on the wall for the patio.

I couldn't believe what I had just heard. I was petrified...so afraid my body was shaking. I needed to get out of there fast. The sun began to rise and I was happy because then I could use my cousin having to go to work, and me having to pick up Lil Carter, as an excuse. I didn't want to make my nervousness obvious so I rolled over and kissed Dre' awake.

"I have to go; my cousin has to work so I have to go get Lil Carter. Thank you for a wonderful evening."

"Ok babe...never a problem."

I proceeded to get out of bed. Dre' grabbed my arm,

"Sky, I think I'm falling in love with you."

I closed my eyes and sighed quietly. I wanted to grab my purse and run to my car and not look back, but if he was what I heard him talking about on the phone, I probably wouldn't even make it to the bedroom door. I turned to him and touched his face.

"Dre,' it's too soon to know. Let's just take it slow. You know my situation is complicated, but trust me, you will be the first to know when I come up with an escape plan."

I got up and headed to the bathroom to put on my clothes and wash my face.

"Do you have any new tooth brushes?" I asked.

"Yes, look in the closet in the bathroom."

After dressing and brushing my teeth, I headed towards the door. Dre' was there waiting for me.

"When will I see you again?"

I had to ask him so that he wouldn't notice my nervousness and become suspicious.

Dre' looked down at me... and at that moment I could see that dark and cold look in his eyes I thought I had seen before.

"Soon...I hope." he responded.

Once I made it to the car, I started crying. What have I gotten myself into? Who is this person? What does he do? Is this why he has all the high tech surveillance cameras and intercom systems at Ms. Loretta's house and his? Why is he talking about killing someone and their child?

I tried to convince myself that I must have heard him wrong, but deep down I knew I heard him correctly. Is that what he meant when he asked me at the hospital if I wanted him to take care of C.J.? I mean he has killed before. Why did he confess that to me though he hardly knows me?

My mind was running a mile a minute and I couldn't stop shaking. I started to feel sick to my stomach. I opened my car door and threw up. The bottom line of it all...I was having sex with a killer.

CHAPTER 12

SILVER LINING

I picked up Lil Carter and then rushed home to shower and make it seem like we had been there all night before C.J. decided to come home. I wasn't sure if he would even come home. When I pulled up to the apartment; as luck would have it, his car was already parked outside.

"Shit!"

"What's wrong, Mommy?"

"Nothing, baby. Listen…if Daddy asks where we have been; tell him we both spent the night at Cousin Theresa's house, ok?" I had to tell him just in case C.J. asked.

"Ok, Mommy."

When we got out of the car and went into the apartment building…the closer I got to our door the more I could smell food cooking and music playing. I was hoping we either had company, or he was in a good mood; either way, I knew he wouldn't try to start a fight or argument.

When I put my key in the door and opened it, sitting at the door was a huge life size teddy bear holding a dozen red roses, and a card. I took the card because I knew this was all for me. The only time C.J. bought me things aside from a birthday or holiday, was after a fight that he knew he was guilty of starting.

I opened the card first. It simply read, "I'm sorry." I smiled, but I knew in my heart that this was only temporary.

C.J. came to the door with a new video game for Lil Carter. He knew exactly how to win back his son's heart. Then he looked at me with those pitifully sad eyes and hugged me.

"Babe, I'm really sorry. I'm going to go for counseling. I promise I'm going to see somebody and get help. I think I have a problem. I promise I will never hurt you again."

Although these were the same words he had recited before, somehow he always reeled me back in. His apology sounded genuine but I knew it wouldn't last long. If I could count how many times he had told me that and get one hundred dollars every time, I would be a fucking billionaire. Needless to say, I wasn't going to complain. C.J. in a good mood was rare. Besides, after that conversation I heard Dre' having on the phone that morning... home was the only place I wanted to be.

Once I put away our things, I showered and slipped on some joggers and a t-shirt.

Whatever C.J was cooking smelled so good that it had my stomach growling.

When I walked in the kitchen to see what it was, C.J. said, "I cooked your favorite; chicken alfredo and garlic bread. I bought some movies to watch too. We can stay in today... just me, you, and Lil Carter."

I didn't have any argument to his suggestion. After last night, I was exhausted. My hope was that C.J. wasn't going to try to have sex because Dre' had me sore as hell and we had sex without a condom...and he...*Ooh my God!!* I thought. *He came in me! Ooh my God! Ooh my God!!*

I panicked! I should have went and got a morning after pill before coming home. There was no way I would be able to go out without C.J. asking questions or worse... going with me. I could just tell him I came on and needed some tampons but I already had a huge box that we picked up at Sam's club last week when we went grocery shopping. Ooh my God, how stupid am I?

I couldn't believe I let this happen.

We stayed in the house the whole day and watched movies. It felt kind of good...like my family was complete.

C.J. fell asleep lying across my lap on the couch. I watched him as he slept. I loved that man so much. It didn't matter the amount of shit he put me through. I couldn't understand how much power he had over me,

He cheated, hit me, disrespected me mentally, verbally, and emotionally, and I still loved him. I couldn't understand it. I'd prayed every day for God to pull me out of that hell I was living in, but when he tried to, I kept going back. *Why do I allow that man to control my heart?* I often thought.

♥♥♥♥♥♥♥♥

Lil Carter and I watched a few more movies. It was getting late so I got ready for bed. I went in the bedroom and grabbed my phone while C.J. was still asleep. I hadn't checked it since I been home.

I had a few missed calls and text from Dre.'

"Sky, we should talk."

"Call me."

"Are you ok?"

As I read the messages, I wondered what he wanted to talk to me about. My heartbeat sped up.

Did he know that I listened to his conversation from the bathroom intercom? Ooh my God...does he have cameras in his bathroom and he went back and watched me listening after I left? What will he do?

I decided to text him back just to get a feel of what he was thinking.

"Yes, I'm fine, but can't talk right now. C.J. is home, and what is it that we need to talk about?"

"Just call me when you have a minute," his text responded.

"Ok, I'll call you tomorrow."

♥♥♥♥♥♥♥♥

I didn't plan on calling him for a couple of weeks if ever again. The things I heard that morning had me second guessing what I was doing. I didn't know exactly what Dre' did for a living and after the conversation I heard I was not sure if I want to know.

The reality was that I did have to fulfill my contract obligation that I had with them cleaning and organizing his grandmother's home in a couple of weeks. I hoped I didn't run into him there. The plan was to get in, do my job, and leave. I was hoping that perhaps he would forget about me and move on. As fine as he was, I know there were a million and one ladies waiting in line to get next to him.

My mind drifted off to the first time we had sex. It was like nothing that I had ever experienced before. My panties got wet at the thought of him, and I questioned whether or not I wanted another women to take my place. I wanted to be loved and adored and that's exactly what Dre' did for me.

How was it that I let myself get caught up with this man that I know nothing about?

I let him tell me his deepest secret that I knew was something that I would have to take to the grave. Thinking about him made me want him even more.

What is it about Dre' that I couldn't let go of? I pondered the thought and the answer was always the same...I don't know.

♥♥♥♥♥♥♥♥

A few weeks had gone by since I had heard from Dre.' C.J. had been staying home and being really helpful around the house and more attentive towards our son. It felt so right because I thought maybe... just maybe we were good now.

He started the anger management classes. I would sometimes go with him for the support.

I was hopeful this would last longer than the last time and the time before that.

CHAPTER 13

I LOVE THEM

I was up early preparing for my job at Ms. Loretta's house. I had to go out and buy plastic bens and organizers because there was a lot of stuff that Ms. Loretta wanted to donate to the homeless shelter. I knew I would be there most of the day so I arranged for Lil Carter to sleep over at my cousin's house where he could play with her son.

When I got to Ms. Loretta's house, I had the key pad number so that I could gain entry. Dre'a had given it to me prior to starting the job. No one was there, which was a relief because I wanted to get started as quickly as possible and the leave quietly.

I started from the basement and worked my way up. I placed everything that would be donated out in the driveway because Dre'a had already arranged for a truck to pick the things up and take them away. As I took a few more items outside, I walked past the closet that Dre' and I first had our sexual encounter. I walked in and stood in the middle of the floor. I closed my eyes and remembered the way he kissed me and fucked me. I was getting moist just thinking about it.

Since I left his house a few weeks ago, I couldn't stop thinking about him. Any smart woman would've run, changed her number, mailed him that check back, and never showed up for the job. That little something about him kept drawing me in and part of me was hopeful. I wanted to be his, and him to be mine.

I secretly wanted him to take care of C.J. for me also. I was aware that it would come at a price. I wouldn't be able to live with myself, having to look at Lil Carter every day and hearing him asking for his dad. I wish I could just run away from all of it...the entire story...C.J., Dre' everything.

I thought about the twenty thousand dollar check Dre' had written me. I could have done many things with it. I could have used the cash to start all over somewhere else... maybe Atlanta. I could grow my business there. I had heard every entrepreneur that moved there had become successful. It looked like the place to be to live the life I wanted.

The reality would set in as I was concerned about Lil Carter possibly resenting me for taking him away from his dad. I had to be conscious of the fact that if I was to go through with that plan, I would be leaving everything behind... taking our personal belongings only. Lil Carter would have to leave everything including his dad. I would have to get my number changed because I knew if C.J. found me; it would be hell to pay. At that point, things had been going great at home with C.J. He had been home more and we had been getting along like no other time before. It had been amazing.

We haven't had sex because C.J. said he wanted me to be able to trust him again. He didn't pressure me for sex. He said he'd wait until I was ready. This effort was to my advantage because I was still a little sore from the sex with Dre'.

I also hadn't been feeling very well at that point. I started my period and it only lasted for 1 day which was weird because normally (for me), it lasted for 5 days. I knew my seasons were changing so I didn't pay it much mind. I had an appointment coming up with my OB/GYN to make sure everything was ok because I had issues in the past with fibroids which often effected my period.

♥♥♥♥♥♥♥♥

As I was walking out of the closet, I heard a car pull up. I figured it was the truck to pick up the donated items out in the driveway. When I walked to the door, I opened it; there was a Black Range Rover pulling into the driveway. In fact...the same one I saw at Dre's condo.

Ugh! I wanted to be done and gone before he came. I thought that avoiding him would prevent me from having to be forced to face our reality...whatever that was at the time. I knew he would want to know why I hadn't called or returned his calls. I also knew I wasn't actually prepared to tell the truth.

He sat in his truck for a while. I was anxiously

awaiting the next scene to play out so I watched and anticipated his reaction, but I couldn't see what he was doing because his windows were tinted. When he stepped out of the truck, his six foot one inch frame over shadowed my previous thoughts.

Dre' had on a brand new pair of Jordan's, hoop shorts, and a tank top. I assumed he must have just come from hooping. Whatever the case was, he was sexy and looking directly at me.

"Hello, Skylar."

The tone of his voice was every indication that he didn't care to speak to me... but did it anyway because it was the polite thing to do.

His cold and unfeeling greeting forced me to feel as if I had to explain.

"Hi, Dre'... I was just finishing up. Now, I am waiting on the truck to come pick up the things Ms. Loretta wants to donate."

"Good! You are welcome to leave now. I can wait on the truck. Thank you for your services Sky, but we have decided to go with another company to maintain the cleaning and laundry for my grandmother. Don't bother returning the rest of the money...like I said, it was a tip. Keep it and go buy you and your family something nice."

I was in shock and I know it showed on my face. I couldn't believe what he was saying. Needless to say, my feelings were hurt a little.

I stood there...feet seemed to be planted into the ground...for a minute with a surprised look on my face. He walked past me and gave me a *leave now* look.

I walked back in the house behind him to retrieve my things and then walked back out to my car. I turned around to look back; he was standing in the doorway. Dre' coldly closed it when I made it to my car. I turned back to get into my car. The tears mounted up in my eyes. Without a shadow of a doubt, I knew this was my fault.

I had been purposely ignoring his calls and text messages. I didn't know why I was crying...couldn't begin to explain it, but *this* was what I wanted originally. We...meaning C.J. and I... were doing better.

I was confused because I still wanted to be with Dre' also.

Fuck this!

I got out of my car, walked back up to the door, and pressed the button on the screen. A few seconds later, his face popped up. When he saw it was me, the door opened by itself, then I walked in. I heard Dre's voice say, "Did you forget something?"

In full fledged tears, "No, I did not. Why are you treating me like this? You knew that I was in a relationship. You knew it, but you didn't care. You still made me want you. You still seduced me."

"Wait! What?" Dre' asked. "Seduced you?" he laughed.

"Skylar, you wanted to fuck just as much as I did...so don't give me that shit!"

Dre' walked close to me. I grew frightened... I wasn't sure what he was getting ready to do. I flinched as he got closer. He froze in his steps and looked at me.

"You really think I would hit you, Sky?" He shook his head in disappointment before walking away.

"Dre,' I'm sorry. It's a reflex, I guess... because you know..."

Cutting me off, "Listen Sky...I will never hit you, so you never have to worry about that from me. I like you a lot...I really do, but I can't just be yo *side nigga* and sit around and watch while he beats you to death. I wanted to help you at first...help you get away from him, but you made me want you. I'm thinking we seduced each other Skylar."

What he was saying was true.

"Look...if you want me to leave...I will, but I do like you a lot Dre.' You have to understand that I'm confused right now. I enjoy you. You're different than C.J. You are nice. We have good conversation... and the sex is amazing...bananas even. The sex makes this more complicated than it needs to be. Give me time...I need time to think. This is moving too fast."

"Sky, I know you like me and I'm not trying to complicate things. I'll give you the time to think if that's what you want."

He said these words prior to walking up to me and

kissing me on the forehead. Dre' pulled my head up with his hand so that I could look up at him,

"I'm here if you need me. Give me a call, ok?"

I nodded my head as to say *ok* and then turned to walk out the door. I paused because I wanted to ask him about that conversation he had on the phone with someone that morning but I decided against it. *I was hoping that maybe I heard it wrong...after all; I couldn't hear the person on the other end of the phone so I may have been tripping,*

Dre' definitely didn't seem to be *that* kind of person. Grant it, he did murder his dad, but he had no choice.

I continued out the door and got into my car and drove away.

CHAPTER 14

SHADES OF BLUE

When I pulled up to the apartment complex, C.J. was outside standing by a car that I didn't recognize. I wondered where Lil Carter was because he texted me earlier and said he picked him up from my Cousin Theresa's house. I figured he must have been inside the apartment.

Dre' was hollering at someone on the inside of the car so I parked nearby. When I got out, I could see that there was a woman inside and he was arguing with her.

"Bitch, you really gonna come to my house where my son lay his head? Are you serious? I can't believe you! I should just slap the fuck outta you!" he threatened.

"Try me, Carter! Try me and I will have your ass right in jail! I'm sick of playing these games with you!" She was livid...and they were both yelling at one another so neither one of them saw me walking up.

"C.J., is everything ok?" I turned to her, "And who is this?"

Sadly, I already knew the answer.

He turned to me with a shocked look on his face. At that point, she looked like she instantly got more pissed off than she already was.

"Oh, is this your bitch, Carter? Is the one you been telling me you ain't fucking with no more... you just come see your son over here? Huh, Carter?"

She had gone from *checking* him to antagonizing him as she kept calling him *Carter* which was odd because the only people that called him that was me, (when I was mad at him) and his family. I was sure she wasn't family because of the statement she made. She obviously had known C.J for a long time and was close enough to know his government name. C.J. *never* told anyone his birth name.

I knew exactly what was happening, but I decided it would be easier to act confused. "C.J, what's going on?"

"Sky, just go in the house...I'll explain later. Lil Carter is inside. I picked him up from Theresa's house earlier."

"Explain what? Carter, tell that bitch what you tell me every night!" she started holler again. Now at this point, I was beginning to get pissed off and it wasn't just at the fact that I knew what was going on. I believe my emotions was geared towards the realization that this bitch knew who I was, and where I slept... and C.J. was not going crazy on her the way I knew he would've done on me if the roles were reversed.

"Ok C.J., who the fuck is she and why is she at our house? Why aren't you explaining this to me in front of her? What? Is it that you don't want her to hear you?"

I demanded answers in the flood of questions.

C.J. turned to look at me with the evilest glare...one of which he didn't at all give *her* when she was screaming at him just a few seconds earlier. He seemed intimidated by her the whole time she was questioning and taunting him.

"Sky, I asked you nicely to go into the house...I'll explain later! Both of yall hoes about to make me slap the fuck outta both of yall!"

Those words must have hit a nerve because the woman jumped out of the car and started swinging on him. Of course, like only his women would do, I started swinging on her for a variety of reasons.

First, you come to my house talking shit to me and C.J. like we came to your house, and then you put your hands on my man. Ooh bitch! I have a bunch of built up frustration and pinned up energy and I been waiting on a bitch to try me. Today is your unlucky day!

 C.J. was standing in the middle of us trying to hold this bitch back. I was swinging over him landing each blow to her face and head. Surprisingly, C.J. turns on me and instead of holding me back like he did her, he started punching me. The first blow was to my face causing me to fall on the ground. The next thing I knew; both C.J. and her were jumping on me. It was a brutal attack.

I couldn't believe it! I felt like I was having a bad dream but then when I realized I wasn't, I wanted to die. I prayed as they were beating me.

"Lord, just take me out of this hell I'm living in. Lord, keep my baby safe. Let my family raise him. I'm tired of him seeing me suffer. He will have a much happier life without me. In a sense, I was praying for death."

I couldn't feel the blows anymore as my body became numb and the sounds were muffled. I remembered trying to get up off the ground after the hitting stopped and hearing a car door close. I couldn't see because blood covered my eyes. I heard the screeching of car tires and *boom*... the girl had struck me with her car while she and C.J. continued fighting.

I laid there on the ground hoping that one of the neighbors would come out and help me. I was light headed. The last thing I remembered was the old lady across the hall from me calling my name.

"Sky... Skylar! Talk to me." she begged.

I was in and out of consciousness.

"Call 911!" she screamed to people standing nearby watching and recording with their cell phones.

She got down on the ground with me and laid my head across her lap.

"The ambulance is on its way, Skylar. You just hold on."

While lying there, I started crying...the tears were not because I was in pain. Some parts of my body felt numb. I wanted to know why God was taking me through this. *What did I do to deserve this? Where was C.J.? Did he leave with her? Why would he do this to me and just leave me here for dead? I couldn't understand...we were getting along so well these past few weeks.*

I couldn't breathe. I was overwhelmed with emotions. *Why God? Why doesn't he love me as much as I love him?*

Next, I heard the sirens approaching, and then the old lady asked me if Lil Carter was in the apartment. I struggled to nod my head *yes* before I blacked out again.

When I came to, I was inside the ambulance...the EMT kept asking me, "Skylar, do you know who would've done this to you?"

In a faint voice, I replied, "Yes... my son's father and some girl that I don't know."

"Is there anyone you want us to call?" was the last thing I heard before I blacked out again for the last time.

When I woke up, it must have been hours later because I was all bandaged and cleaned up, and lying in a hospital bed, there was a nurse standing next to me checking my vital signs.

"Hello, Skylar you're in Providence Hospital. Can you remember why you're here?" she asked.

When I tried to move my neck to follow the sound of her voice; I couldn't. I was wearing some type of brace around it. I could hardly speak, so I just nodded my head *yes*.

"Your boyfriend is here. It turns out that your neighbor got the number out of your cell phone because it was the last missed call. He came right away to the hospital."

My eyes got big....she sensed something was wrong. My lips were swollen so I could hardly speak.

"I'll get him for you, Skylar... just a minute," and she walked out of the room. She probably thought I wanted C.J. to come into the room, but I was actually trying to get her attention to tell her he was the one that did this to me and to please do not let him near me... then I heard her call his name.

"Dre', excuse me... Dre', Skylar is woke now."

When I heard her call him, I was surprised, confused, and relieved. I was surprised that he cared enough to come see about me...confused as to why Dre' was there acting as my boyfriend, and relieved that C.J. was not on the premises.

I was baffled as to why Dre' was calling me when this was happening because I had just left him.

When he entered the room, he had a *pissed off* look on his face...like he wanted to strangle somebody.

"Dre', where is my baby? Where is Lil Carter?" I whispered.

"Your neighbor went and got him out of the apartment. She also retrieved your things off the ground..."

I interrupted. "...and she called you?"

"... and she wasn't sure who to call so she called the last missed call from your phone which was me." He continued, "I came right over to the hospital when she told me what happened. Lil Carter is with my grandmother and sister. Don't worry about him Sky, he is in good hands."

I knew Ms. Loretta would take good care of Lil Carter because, although I met her once, she gave off the warm and loving vibes that any grandmother would.

"Skylar, listen... I know you're going to try and fight me on this, but you can't keep letting this lame nigga do this to you. Do you realize that he just jumped on you with one of his bitches and then let the bitch hit you with her car! Enough is enough! What! Do you want this nigga to kill you?" he shouted.

I could see the fire in his eyes.

I closed my eyes because I knew what Dre' was saying was true and I didn't want to face it or him. I couldn't believe any of this was happening. I wanted it to be a bad dream but the pain I was feeling was confirmation that it wasn't. I don't know which hurt worse... the physical pain or the emotional pain I was experiencing knowing that this was all at the hands of the man I loved...the one I shared so much history with... the father of my only son.

♥♥♥♥♥♥♥♥

The Doctor that was treating me walked into the room. "Hello, Skylar. I'm Dr. Amad. You were brought in by ambulance and they gave me the information about what happen to you. Most of your injuries were minor scrapes and bruises, and a lot of swelling. Unfortunately, you do have a fractured rib and broken arm... which are stable. However, you will have a little soreness over the next few months until they are healed completely. I did order a full body MRI to make sure you didn't have any internal bleeding or bruises... and you don't. On the downside, you do have a ruptured disk in your lower back. This may have been from the car hitting you. Have you had any problems in the past with your back, or been in a car accident before?"

"No. Not at all." I answered,

"Ok, I guess it's safe to say this is probably a result of the car hitting you. Let me show you a model of your spine and disk so that you get a closer look and a better understanding."

The Doctor pulled out what looked to be a spine and then showed me how our bodies are built, what the disk holds in place, what they look like when they are damaged, and how it affects the back (pain wise).

I couldn't believe that this happened to me. I could have been paralyzed or worse...killed....and for *what?*

"It's not a major problem, but you are going to need to

see a back specialist and a physical therapist to manage your pain and help you regain physical ability... like walking upright. Other than that, you should be fine. We are going to keep you for a few more days and monitor you. I have some counselor's coming to speak with you because of the type of trauma you went through. There is also a psychiatrist coming to consult you. Again, Skylar... you are in good hands here at Providence Hospital and we will discharge you in a few days. I'm so sorry this had to happen to you," Dr. Amad said as he was leaving the room.

Tears slowly streamed down my face.

"Dre', can you ask your sister to bring my son up here. I need to see him... make sure he is ok?"

"Sky, you need to get some sleep and rest. Lil Carter doesn't need to see you like this."

Dre' made sense but I didn't want to see that.

"No Dre,' I won't be able to rest until I see my baby. He won't be able to sleep until he sees me," I said angrily.

"Ok Sky... Ok, I'll call her now," he said and stepped out into the hallway to speak on the phone. When he came back in into the room, he had a serious look on his face.

"What?" I asked.

"Nothing... she's on the way with Lil Carter."

That was a relief because I needed my baby. I wouldn't

be able to rest until I knew he was ok...somewhat comfortable, and not scared and worried for me.

"Dre,' I'm sorry for having to put you in the middle of all this. It was not my intention. I'm so confused...I don't know what to do. Should I press charges? Should I just let it go? I don't know. I don't understand why he treats me like this. I love him. I'm his son's mother. What did I do to deserve this?"

I became emotional and couldn't stop the tears. I felt like I couldn't breathe.

Dre' walked over and sat on my bed, "Sky, listen you will never understand why he does what he does. My mom never did anything to my dad to deserve what he would do to her. He wouldn't let her work and I think it was because he wanted to control her. She was a *stay at home* mom...she would cook, clean and do everything under the sun for us and my father. He would come home mad because one of his hoes or somebody at work pissed him off and he would take it out on my mom. He was just an unhappy person. When he was beating her, he had this look in his eyes like he wanted her dead. I'll never forget that look. It's embedded in my soul. He killed her and tortured her just like he wanted. She begged him not to hurt us. I believe my mom knew he was going to kill her. I think she believed he was going to kill all of us that night (including himself) and I wasn't going to let that happen. I was only fourteen years old and had never thought about killing anyone, but it was like something or somebody took over my body and mind. When I went to get that gun, I wasn't going to let him get away with taking her from us. He's not going to stop Sky. I *know* that you know what needs to be done."

I looked Dre' right in the eyes and I could see that scared little fourteen year old boy turned killer. He had an instinct to kill or be killed...and it scared me, but at the same time, turned me on. I knew if I was his, he would go to any extent to protect me...even if it meant murder.

♥♥♥♥♥♥♥♥

My family had begun to come to the hospital to see me. My aunt was fuming when she got there. I could almost see the smoke coming from her ears. She absolutely hated C.J. because she knew all the things he's done to me over the years. In the past, I had run away to her house when things got bad.

She was my mom's baby sister and when my mom passed away, she stepped up to the plate so I would call her auntie/mommy. She also knew all about Dre' and liked him based on what she heard. She wanted me to be careful with my heart...reminding me that just as C.J. started out as my best friend then progressed to my lover. *Who would've thought he turn to being what he had become?*

I thought that C.J. must have called his brother and sent him to check on me at the hospital when I saw him walk into my hospital room.

"Sky, what the fuck...? What happened?" he asked. I thought he was trying to play dumb, but I knew C.J.

filled him in otherwise he wouldn't have been there.

Corey and I were really close... almost like real siblings. I could talk to him about anything...especially since he expressed how much he hated how C.J. would treat me. I was no idiot...fully aware that C.J. was still his brother and that's where his loyalty lies... with his blood. *Blood is thicker than water.*

♥♥♥♥♥♥♥♥

"Corey, don't play dumb with me. I know your brother told you what him and his bitch did to me!"

"Yeah well, my Moms told me...not him. I been looking for his hoe ass for two hours now. He called Moms bugging out about what happened. He's all scared that he is going to jail."

"Is that why you're here...to convince me not to send your brother to jail?" I said with an angry look on my face.

"Hell naw! I came to make sure you and Lil Carter were ok. That was some hoe shit they did and to be one hundred with you, Ima beat that nigga ass when I see him. You're his son's mother; there's no way in hell he should've did you like this."

As Corey was finishing what he was saying, Dre' walked back into the room. Corey was sitting on my hospital bed so Dre' looked at me with concern.

"Is everything ok, Sky?" he said,

"Yes, this is C.J.'s brother, Corey. Corey, this is Dre;'

one of my clients," I said while looking at Dre'.

Clearly, he was not happy with the *bullshit* line I fed Corey but it was for the best. Dre' had this "*a client? Yeah right*" look on his face.

I couldn't believe the look on Dre's face when I introduced him as a client, but after all... that's really what we were considered.

"What up?" Dre' said as he extended his hand to Corey.

"What's up?" Corey said with a look on his face like *really client?*

Dre' noticed that look and explained why he was there. This was surprising and necessary.

"Skylar called to let me know that she was done with the cleaning of my grandmother's house and leaving the estate. Her neighbor got her things...including her phone when this attack took place...and since I was the last number in the call log, she called me and explained what happened. I didn't know who to call so I came down to make sure she was ok. My sister and grandmother have Lil Carter...trust that he's in good hands and on his way here with them."

Corey looked at me. "Oh ok, that's cool. Thanks, my guy for checking on her... I got it from here."

Corey wasn't sure if he believed what Dre' said or not but he kept his comment to himself and I was certain that he made a mental note to talk to C.J. about the meeting of this client/*comfortable* stranger.

"I really appreciate this and I'm sure Sky does too... and please thank your sister and grandmother for looking after my nephew for *us*," Corey said before walking Dre' to the door to usher him out of my room.

Dre' looked at me and I didn't know what to say. I knew he wanted me to tell Corey that we had slept together based upon his facial expression but that was not the time or the place for his confessions. The real issue was what had just happened to me, and the whereabouts of my son.

"Yes Dre,' I really appreciate this. Thank you so much."

I made that statement not knowing what else to say, and to keep my cover from being blown.

Dre' walked toward the door without saying a word. I could see he was upset. Just then, in walks Lil Carter with Dre'a.

"MOMMY MOMMY! What happened? Why would Daddy do this? I'm scared."

I felt bad because I knew I could take him out of that situation but I was afraid of him resenting me for leaving C.J. I also knew how important it was to Lil Carter to have both parents in the house. I didn't want Lil Carter to feel like he had to choose between us, but I also knew that this wasn't healthy for him and by no means was I going to risk Lil Carter growing up to be the kind of man that thinks he can disrespect and put his hands on a women. I would die first before I allowed that to happen. He was nine years old so I needed to start now before it was too late.

♥♥♥♥♥♥♥♥

It was times like this when I felt alone; I didn't have anyone to turn to.

After thanking Dre'a for keeping Lil Carter safe, she and Dre' left the room. Lil Carter sat down and began watching cartoons.

"So, who was that nigga, Sky? The way he looked at you didn't seem like he was just a *client*." Corey said, with a *cut the bullshit* look on his face.

I damn sure wasn't going to tell him the truth about Dre' if that's what he was thinking.

"Dre' is my client. Corey, why would I lie? The neighbor called the last number on my call list which just so happened to be Dre'. She must have panicked. I don't know...I was just as surprised as you are when I saw Dre' here."

The fact that she handled it the way she did only made sense, but my guilty conscious paired with Corey's suspicions was trying to ruin things.

Corey looked at me, "Ok, well I'll be back. I have to go check to see if anyone has heard from C.J. again. Take care sis, maybe I'll come back tomorrow to check on you."

I was relieved that he was gone because I didn't want to discuss me and Dre' anymore. I laid back and smiled at the thought of Dre' coming to check on me so fast after my neighbor had called him.

Dre'a walked back into the room after she saw Corey leave.

"Hey, I thought you left with your brother?"

"No, I wanted to stay behind and talk to you. Sky, I know we don't know each other that well but my brother tells me everything. Listen...you need to get out of that relationship with your son's father. It's not healthy for Lil Carter or for you. I'm sure Dre' told you about our mother. I loved my dad but he never changed. For as long as I can remember, he beat on our mom...it didn't stop until he killed her that night. He stripped us of our lives...for Dre'... his sanity *and* childhood. Dre' is really sensitive to your situation. He literally hates men like C.J. I'm telling you...don't fool yourself, it won't get better," she warned.

I knew what Dre'a was saying was true and I needed to leave as soon as possible, but I was scared of what would happen after I left. *Where would I go? How would I keep C.J. from finding me? What could I tell Lil Carter to make him understand?* All these thoughts were going through my head and I couldn't turn them off.

"I know Dre'a... I'm confused."

"Well Sky, I'm here for you... we all are. Trust me; we know firsthand how you feel. If there's anything we can do to help just, say the word."

"Thank you...actually; there is one thing I really need. Is it possible that you and Ms. Loretta can keep Lil

Carter until they discharge me? C.J. knows where all my family lives and he might try to take Lil Carter to get to me. I promise I'll come for him as soon as the Doctor's discharge me."

"Of course we will, Sky... and you have nothing to worry about. We will take good care of him, and I'll bring him to see you every day."

Her smile was confirmation enough.

"Thank you so much, Dre'a. You guys are truly a blessing."

♥♥♥♥♥♥♥♥

I was in the hospital for the next four weeks. I had to go to physical therapy every day until I was discharged. While I was in the hospital, my aunt went to file charges against C.J. She had the officers come to get a statement from me. A judge granted a PPO, and put a warrant out for the arrest of C.J. and the woman that hit me with her car.

♥♥♥♥♥♥♥♥

I was watching the news waiting to be discharged and that woman's picture came up on the screen. Her body was found in her house. Reporters said it looked like she was shot in the head. I couldn't believe what I was seeing.

C.J. was also missing. His family hadn't heard from him, but I figured he was just on the run because of the warrant the judge granted for his arrest in connection with the assault.

I sat up in my bed feeling sick as I hoped and prayed that C.J. didn't do this. I didn't want to believe he was capable of killing anyone but *where could he be?*

Corey went to our apartment and saw that most of his clothes were gone, but some important things were left behind. That struck us as unusual *if* he was actually on the run. I figured he probably would come back once everything died down but now the woman was dead. This detail changed the dynamics of the situation. There was no true escape.

My mind was all over the place. I thought of how angry Dre' was seeing what happened to me. *No, it couldn't have been Dre.' He wouldn't have killed that girl.* On the other hand, I didn't know that for sure. *How would he even know who she was?* Dre' came to visit me every day and usually stayed all day, morning, noon and night. He only left to go home and change clothes and take care of some business but I had no idea what type of business it was. Dre' walked in just as I was turning off the TV.

"You ready to roll?" he asked. When I didn't answer, he looked at me, "Are you ok, Sky?"

"Yes, I'm fine...just a little sore."

Dre and I had agreed that me and Lil Carter staying at his condo was the best thing for us...at least until I figured out what I was going to do. He had someone go move my things from the apartment and put them into storage. The Leasing Office allowed me to terminate my lease. My plan was to only stay with Dre' until I was well enough to care for myself and Lil Carter.

CHAPTER 15

LOYAL TO THE GAME

Dre'

I walked into the abandoned house that I grew up in shortly after I had dropped Sky off at the condo. After what she had gone through, I wanted her to be comfortable so Dre'a and my grandmother were there keeping her company. Dre'a decided to cook a *welcome home* dinner for Sky. Before leaving, I told them I would be back after paying the movers that packed and moved Sky's things out of her apartment.

♥♥♥♥♥♥♥

I walked to the basement door and listened for any movement from C.J. I didn't hear anything. I thought about how easy it was to get C.J. In fact, in my line of work, he was the perfect target. I sat outside of Skylar's house every day because I knew his lame ass would come back there to get some of his shit. He was one stupid nigga. I sat there and waited until C.J. returned to the car he pulled up in. I followed him to see where he was laying his head at night. It was no surprise to find that it was at the bitch house who hit Sky with her car. I parked and watched her house everyday to get familiar with their daily routine. I saw them fighting and arguing, but the girl was usually the one fighting C.J. For some reason, he wouldn't hit her like he hit Sky. I tried but I couldn't figure out why. I knew I was going to have to off that bitch immediately because she was a little feisty but I didn't care because she was just in the way and I wanted C.J. so I could kidnap, torture, and then watch his sorry ass die a slow death.

♥♥♥♥♥♥♥♥

Just as Mr. Santiago instructed, the next night I waited until they were asleep and slipped inside the house. For some odd reason, this dumb hoe always left her patio porch unlocked.

♥♥♥♥♥♥♥♥

I screwed the silencer on my 9mm and walked to the bedroom where C.J. and the girl were asleep. I wore all black...all you could see was the whites of my eyes. Once in the bedroom, I knew exactly what side she slept on because I came in before to see if she had any pets while they were asleep. I fired a shot hitting her in the back of the head. Her body flinched but it didn't move enough to wake C.J. I walked over to his side of the bed and put the gun in his mouth. He attempted to jump up until he saw the gun and then me standing over him...he froze. C.J. looked over at the girl and saw the back of her head was oozing with blood. I was sure he knew he wasn't going to make it out alive. C.J. had to have known it would only be a matter of time before Mr. Santiago was going to send someone to kill him. C.J. tried to plead, but I wasn't hearing that shit.

"Man please...I have a son and a girl. Please don't kill me. Did Mr. Santiago send you? I have most of his money...I swear. Please man!"

He knew death was near just as I knew he didn't have the money. I wanted to off him right then and there for crying like a little bitch, but Mr. Santiago gave me specific instructions that I would have to carry out.

I hit C.J. with the butt of the gun knocking him out. Then I carried him to the van that I was driving, tied him up, and drove him to the abandon house I once called home.

I stood at the top of the stairs shaking my head after thinking about how easy it was to get C.J. I couldn't understand how niggas be so careless with their lives. It's so easy now a day to touch niggas. I walked down the basement stairs and got sick to my stomach by the smell. It was horrible. The scent came from C.J. pissing and shitting on himself mixed with his blood. I had to cover and shield both my mouth and nose.

When I looked at C.J., I smirked because he kind of looked like Sky looked when I first met her in the hospital after he beat her up to the point you couldn't recognize her... but C.J. looked worse. *It ain't no fun when the rabbit got the gun.* Karma is a bitch!

I had already spoken to Mr. Santiago and he sent one

of his men over to make sure C.J. was actually there. I left one of the windows unlocked for his henchman to get in and check things out.

Now I had the confirmation I needed to kill this nigga. I was excited at the thought of having him out of the way soon, but then again, kind of sad because then I would have to make the decision as to kill Sky and Lil Carter. *How could I do it?* Sky and Lil Carter living in the condo would make it easier but I knew I didn't want it to be as violent as Mr. Santiago had instructed. *Perhaps...maybe I will just kill them in their sleep or poison them.* I started to get angry just thinking about it because I loved Skylar.

C.J. began to wake up and was moving around in the chair he was tied to...moaning miserably. I looked at him and felt rage...unspeakable rage because if it wasn't for C.J. not being able to keep his hands to himself and beating Sky, I would have never met Sky that way. I would've just come to kill them without even knowing their situation. Because of what happened to my mother and because of niggas like this and my dad, I became this person... a killer and a hit man.

The number one rule to the game is that killers aren't supposed to feel. It was too late for me...I now cared, loved and felt sympathy for Skylar. I was pissed so I used that moment as his final. I screwed the silencer on my 9mm then aimed it at him. I didn't have a mask on this time so C.J. could see threw the one eye of his that wasn't swollen.

♥♥♥♥♥♥♥♥

C.J.

I recognized *the nigga from the hospital with the old lady that was talking to Sky, and the nigga my brother showed me the picture of that was at the hospital with Sky. All this time, I thought this was someone sent to kill me by Mr. Santiago. It was my own bitch... my son's mother had sent a nigga to off me. How could I have been so stupid? I guess the saying is true, "when a woman's fed up, there's nothing you can do about it."* I closed my eyes and braced myself.

Dre'

I looked at him with no remorse because I saw my father sitting in that chair. The first shot was to C.J.s' stomach. I wanted him to know exactly where each shot was coming from so I painted a narrative for him.

"This one is for Mr. Santiago."

It was written all over his face that C.J. heard me and couldn't believe what he was hearing. I gave him a few seconds to ponder his thought and work through his confusion before I got the pleasure of putting another bullet in his chest.

"This one is for my mother."

The last shot was to his head. After C.J. slumped over, I took a deep breath before concluding, "And that's for Skylar."

It was getting late and I knew I had to get back to the

house to check on Sky so I left C.J. there and would come back the next morning to dispose of his body.

CHAPTER 16

KILLER INSTINCTS

I was out of the hospital for a while and couldn't figure out why C.J. hadn't called to at least check on his son. It wasn't like him to do that...even after a big fight. It wasn't that I wanted to talk to him, but I was still worried for some odd reason.

I stood in the mirror looking at myself...most of my wounds and bruises had healed. I still found it difficult to move around because of my back but it was getting better. I heard a ding and thought it was my phone but mine was in my back pocket. The sound came from the bedroom. When I walked out the bathroom, I could see the light shining from Dre's phone on the night stand. He had three phones and I was thinking that he must have forgotten one. I walked over to the bedroom door and closed it so that Dre'a or Ms. Loretta wouldn't walk in and see me looking through his phone. When I picked it up, I saw a text message from someone named Mr. Santiago. I had no idea who that was but the message read, "I see you obeyed my orders. That nigga owed me a lot of money and he deserved everything you did to him. I hope we have an understanding about the rest of them. Remember, you have until tomorrow to get rid of his body and take care of that other thing."

I couldn't believe what I was reading. I grew nauseous to the point where I felt like I was going to throw up but I continued to investigate. I went to his inbox messages to read more, and there were pictures and an address sent to the same contact...this *Santiago* person. I strolled down to look at the pictures and dropped the phone when I saw the picture of C.J. all beaten up and tied to a chair in what looked like a basement. I ran into the bathroom and threw up. I couldn't believe what I was seeing. *Oh my God, I have to get us out of here.*

So many things were running through my head. I didn't want to believe this but I saw it with my own eyes. I couldn't leave right then because Dre' was probably on his way home and I didn't have my car.

Oh God, what have I done? Who is Dre'? Who is Santiago? Why did C.J. owe him money?

My mind was all over the place, I thought about C.J. *Oh my God, my poor baby! What did they do to him?*

There was an address. I jumped up from leaning over the toilet and went by the bed and picked up the phone. After finding a piece of paper and pen, I wrote down the address and deleted the last message so that when Dre' came home, it wouldn't look like I had read the message. I placed the phone back on the nightstand and walked into the guest bathroom in the hall. I shut and locked the door and slid down onto the floor in tears. I covered my mouth to muffle the sound of my cries so that Dre'a, Ms. Loretta, and Lil Carter wouldn't hear me. I pondered on what to do. *Should I flee... just take Lil Carter and run? What if Dre' finds us? What would he do to us? God, why is this happening to me?*

My mind went back to the phone conversation I heard Dre' having that morning. *Oh God was...he going to kill me and Lil Carter? Were we who he was talking about? But why would he have sex with me? Why wouldn't he just kill me all the times he was alone with me? Why wouldn't he have killed Lil Carter by now?*

That thought alone of Lil Carter made me sick and I moved over to the toilet and threw up again. I have to get my baby out of there. I had to go to that address and untie C.J. We needed to get out of there. It was now apparent that Dre' killed the girl on the news that hit me. I didn't want to believe all the thoughts that were running threw my head but it was obvious.

I had to try to talk myself into being rational and regaining my composure. *Ok, ok I have to stay calm or Dre' will sense something is wrong.* I stood up and put the paper with the address in my pocket.

When I opened the bathroom door, Dre' was standing face to face with me. "Are you ok, Sky?" he asked.

I tried to stay calm, "Yes, I'm good babe...just a little nauseous from the pain medication...that's all. How was your day?" I said. While thinking, *who did you kill today?*

"It was good. I see my sister put Lil Carter to sleep. Let's go take a shower together." he said.

I knew exactly what Dre' wanted and with all that was going on and what I just found out, sex was the last thing on my mind, but it was like something takes over my body and mind when he's around. He puts some type of voodoo on me and I just can't resist temptation.

He took my hand and led me to the bathroom inside his bedroom. As he undressed me, my body was trembling but I didn't want him to stop. Even though I was afraid of him, my body craved him.

Dre' looked down at me, "I love you."

I was on a sexual high and didn't even realize what he had said. Dre' knew exactly where to touch me and exactly where to kiss me...and I loved it.

Dre' led me to the shower, grabbed the back of my neck and my face, and he kissed me like he was never going to let me go. It was something about his touch; how gentle he was with me. I knew he would never hurt me. He laid me down on the shower floor as the water was running all over me and down my face. Dre' kneeled down, lifted my legs in the air, and kissed me starting from my inner thigh up to my foot. My body was trembling even though the water was hot. Dre' looked at me and I think deep down, he knew that I knew everything but he was going to make me forget about it. His tongue circled the inside of my thigh then down to my clitoris and he kissed and sucked it until I felt like I was going to explode. When he moved back up towards me, he said, "Sky I love you."

"Dre,' I love you too."

He made love to me on the shower floor. As much as I wanted him to stop, I didn't want him to stop. I loved every minute...every stroke. As scared and confused as I was I let him do it again. He seduced me, and he was good at it.

I lay in Dre's arms that night. *What the hell am I doing? This man is a killer and I think he is going to kill me* but I wasn't sure of it. At any rate, that should've been enough for me to run.

It was in his eyes. The way he looked at me, kissed me, held me, and made love to me, made me feel like he would never do anything to harm me.

♥♥♥♥♥♥♥

The next morning, I woke up early while Dre' was still asleep. I went into the other room and grabbed Lil Carter's shoes and jacket. I kneeled down on the side of the bed and whispered to Lil Carter to wake up. When he woke up, I had him put his shoes and jacket on and told him to wait by the door. I had to go back into Dre's room to get the paper out of my other pants pocket that I wrote the address on. I picked up my pants and got the small piece of paper out. Dre' turned over, "You're woke early, babe."

"I have to go to physical therapy and I would like to drop Lil Carter off to my cousin's house. He's been through a lot in the past few weeks. I just want him to go have fun and be a kid," I said nervously. Even though I was dropping him off to my cousin's, my honest intention for my destination was different. Dre' didn't need to know that.

I had to go see if what I saw in Dre's phone was true. As much as I hated C.J. for what he and that bitch did to me, I still loved him. Any normal woman would be on the first thing smoking away from both C.J. and Dre,' but I didn't know what it was about me and the men I loved.

Theresa was standing in the door waiting for me. I explained to her over the phone on the way over, what happened. She kept trying to talk me out of it but I knew what I had to do. As we walked up to the door, my cousin gave me a look.

"What Theresa?"

"Why the fuck do you care if that bastard is beat up or dead? Whatever he got...the fucker deserved it! All the times he hurt you Skylar..." she said with tears in her eyes.

"It's not that easy to walk away Theresa. It's easier said than done." I kissed Lil Carter on his forehead and kissed Theresa on the cheek.

"I'll be back...I promise."

I walked off the porch and got back into Dre's Range Rover. I pulled out the slip of paper with the address on it and put it into the GPS on my phone. I turned on the location services on my phone just in case something happened and gave Theresa the password to my find my iPhone account.

CHAPTER 17

EPIPHANY

After driving for about forty-five minutes, I pulled on to a dirt road where a big old house sat. The house looked like it belonged in the south. It had one of those porches that wrapped around the whole house. It looked nice but some of the windows were boarded up so I knew no one was living there.

When I got out of the truck and walked up to the door, I got an eerie and cold feeling. The door was locked but there was a window slightly open on the side of the house just beyond the porch. I climbed inside that window. Luckily, the sun was coming up; otherwise the house would have been dark.

I called out C.J.'s name but didn't get an answer. I walked around the whole house...still no sign of C.J., and then it dawned on me. According to the picture on the phone, he was in a basement so I went into the kitchen and found the basement door. The door made a creaking noise...like an old haunted house. I covered my nose and mouth because there was a really bad stench coming from the basement. As I walked down the stairs, I used the flashlight on my phone to lead me through a clear path; however, there were windows that allowed some light shine in. As I came closer to meeting the bottom of the stairs, the smell got worse. I stopped and prayed to God that it wasn't C.J. that I smelled.

"Lord, please...I know what he did to me was bad, but Lil Carter needs him."

Tears filled my eyes at the thought because I knew what I was about to see but for some reason, I needed to see it with my own eyes.

I made it to the bottom of the stairs and shined my phone light straight ahead. There was a chair and someone tied to it. He was slumped over. I cried aloud and covered my mouth. "C.J," I said through sobs, but he didn't move or respond. My whole body was shaking.

I walked toward him and when I walked around to the front of him, my heart felt like it was beating in my throat. I was staring at his lifeless body in a chair. C.J. had been beaten so badly his head was swollen. In fact, I couldn't even recognize who he was. I fell to my knees and cried hysterically. Even though I couldn't recognize him, I knew it was C.J. by the portrait tattoo of Lil Carter on his forearm, and his other tattoos.

I cried and screamed at C.J. like he could hear me.

"Why? Why C.J.? How could you do this to us? How

could you be so stupid? Who was this man you owed money to? What the fuck C.J.? Now me and Lil Carter's life is in danger? What am I supposed to do without you?"

I was so angry at him for letting this happen. I didn't know what I was going to tell Lil Carter, or how I would be able to raise him on my own. I couldn't believe it was true.

Why am I so stupid? How could I have gotten involved with someone like Dre'?

I was crying so hard I never heard a car pull up and the door open.

♥♥♥♥♥♥♥♥

Dre'

When I came back to dispose of C.J.'s body, my Range Rover was parked out front. I was shocked. This could only mean one thing.

What the fuck! How did she find this place? Uggh! Why would she come here? Now this is going to complicate things. I might be forced to kill her now.

I could only blame myself after I realized how sloppy I was with pacing myself and keeping things out of Sky's view. I had left the cell phone out and that was all it would take for her to see everything. I was a professional and part of this line of business is being accurate and clean.

I was in a catch twenty two. She knew too much and I

couldn't risk her running to the police. I would have to follow the original orders from Mr. Santiago which meant I would have to kill the kid also. I loved Sky but I was wise enough to know it would be all bad if he kept her alive now.

I got out of the car and screwed the silencer on the gun and then walked up to the porch and noticed the door hadn't been opened. I was confused as to how she had gotten in the house. I spotted an open window and remembered I left it unlocked for one of Mr. Santiago's men. That idiot forgot to lock it back. I climbed in the window and when I stepped down onto the floor; it creaked...

Sky

I heard it. I stopped crying and covered my mouth. *Oh my God! Who could that be? It was so early in the morning. Dre' couldn't have made it here this fast.*

I looked around for somewhere to hide and I found a dark space in the wall and climbed inside. I prayed and held my breath as I heard footsteps of someone coming down the stairs. I felt like I was going to faint. I could see the bottom half of this person's body. It was Dre', I almost pissed myself when I saw the gun with a silencer in his hand. All I could do was pray.

Lord please let me make it out of here alive, Lil Carter needs me.

Dre' called out my name, "Skylar!"

I held my breath, hoping and praying he would leave. He took out his cell phone and dialed a number and my phone started ringing and lighting up causing me to jump and scream.

Fuck! I hadn't thought to put my phone on silent.

"Dre', please don't hurt me. Please... my baby needs me," pleading with him as I was still inside the crawl space.

He walked over to where I was and pulled me out by my hair then pulled my head back and put the gun in my mouth. I cried harder hoping he would feel some type of remorse and let me go.

"Dre' please," I tried to mumble with the gun in my mouth.

We were face to face and he was looking down at me. I looked into his eyes and could see the coldness that I thought I would see when looking at him, but so many times dismissed it because I knew what he had gone through as a child.

Dre'

I looked into her terrified yet saddened eyes as the river of tears rolled down her face. Although I knew I had to do what I had to do, I was hesitant. There was no denying it...I had fallen in love with Sky and wished she would have just stayed in bed this morning. It was too late to play the blame game. Our reality was standing there and staring me square in my eyes.

Sky

I thought of my baby and I was sure that I couldn't

leave him to live alone in this cold ass cruel world without either of his parents. I had to fight. I would say and do anything to make it out alive.

Dre'

I knew that Skylar loved me. Before this moment, I could feel it in her touch, and hear it in her voice but on this day, I could see it in her eyes. She was just as afraid as I was. I couldn't bear to watch her drown in our emotions so I looked away. She used this as an opportunity to knee me in my groin.

Sky

Dre' grabbed his crouch in pain with the hand he was using to hold me by my hair but he never dropped the gun. I darted for the stairs. After I placed my foot on the first step, I heard a noise and then I felt a horrible burning sensation in my side...and then I saw blood. Without a doubt, I knew that Dre' had shot me. I looked to him until our eyes met. As I fell back onto the stairs I said, "Dre', you promised me you wouldn't ever hurt me. Why?"

Dre'

I looked at Sky staring blankly back at me. I had killed before but this time was different. I didn't mean to shoot her but it was my instincts. I lost control.

I slowly crawled over to her and lifted her head and cradled it in my lap.

"Sky, I'm sorry? Why did you have to do that?

♥♥♥♥♥♥♥♥

Sky

I blacked out and my life flashed before my eyes. I had seen this kind of thing in the movies but now it was happening to me. I saw events that had happened in my life. The one that stood out the most was when I was in the hospital having my baby. That was the best day of my life. I also kept seeing a building that looked to be a church flashing before me. I was standing in the middle of the empty church and at that moment, God spoke to me. I could hear him clear as day... as if he was standing right next to me.

"My child, it's time to come home with me."

"Lord, please, not now. I'm not ready. My baby needs me. Please Lord! Please!" I pleaded.

I hoped the tears streaming down my face would matter.

"My child, so many times I pulled you out of that relationship with C.J. and you kept disobeying me and going back only to be hurt by him again and again. I also showed you signs warning you to stay away from Dre'. I spoke to you and you weren't ready to hear me. Whenever you called on me, I listened and I answered your prayers. I'm always right by your side, but you chose these men over me and the plan I had for you."

I began to think about all the warning signs I was getting about C.J. and Dre' and at that moment, I had an Epiphany. I could remember hearing God speak, but I wasn't ready to hear him so I kept ignoring the signs and making excuses. All this time... all I needed to do was be obedient to God and he would bring peace in my life.

"I'm sorry Lord. Please forgive me. I was so confused and broken I didn't know right from wrong."

"I will always forgive you and keep you, my child, but the next time, listen to my voice when I'm speaking to you."

At that moment, I opened my eyes. Dre' was sitting with his back to me crying. I didn't know how long I had been knocked out, but by the looks of it, Dre' thought I was dead. His gun was lying next to me on the step. I picked it up slowly and fired a shot to his back, he slumped over and I shot him about five times to make sure he was dead. I cried so hard I could hardly see and I just closed my eyes, I had never used or touched a gun before but I knew I had to make it out of there alive.

"Lord, I'm sorry. Please forgive me; for I have sinned."

To Be Continued..............

EPIPHANY Part 2 coming soon!

Andre'a T. Robinson

Contact Information:
Email: andreatrobinson2010@yahoo.com
Facebook: https://www.facebook.com/Epiphany-Forgive-Me-
Lord-For-I-Hve-Sinned-447506935455475
Twitter: AndreaTRobinson
Instagram: AndreaTRobinson

Andre'a T. Robinson

Made in the USA
Charleston, SC
06 January 2016